Everyone Gets Married in the End

Everyone Gets Married in the End

And Other Short Stories

by

JACK WEYLAND

Published by
Horizon Publishers
A division of Cedar Fort Inc.
www.cedarfort.com

Second Printing: November 2004

ISBN: 0-88290-750-6

Printed and distributed
in the United States of America by

Mailing Address:
925 S. Main
Springville, Utah 84663

Local Phone: (801) 489-4084
Toll Free: 1 (800) SKYBOOK
FAX: (801) 489-1097

E-mail: skybook.com
Website: http://www.cedarfort.com

Contents

Everyone Gets Married in the End

My first calling in a campus ward winter semester, just after my mission, was to be one of two home evening group leaders.

"Michael," the counselor in the bishopric said when extending the call, "you'll be working with Heather Andrus. Do you know her?"

"I don't know anyone in the ward. I'm really busy this semester."

"She's a nice girl. Oh, one more thing, in the past, some have called them home evening moms and dads. We're trying to get away from that. We're certainly not calling you and Heather to be a dad and a mom over your home evening group. We're calling you to be leaders. Anyway, get together with Heather. I'm sure you'll enjoy working with her."

After sacrament meeting Heather and I got together to correlate. I was pretty much all business. That's the way I've always been. Because of that, I really didn't pay any attention to her physical appearance, except that her hair, which is either light brown or blonde depending on the light, is straight, except near the ends where it flares out. She has green eyes, and when she's talking to you she maintains eye contact.

I decided that, in general, eye contact is a good thing, and made a mental note to increase eye contact with others by thirty percent within the next thirty days.

I also found out she was waiting for a missionary named Russ.

As the semester progressed, I discovered that my calling didn't take much time, which was good because I had a difficult course dealing with organizational practices in business.

At one of our home evenings in March, Alicia, a junior, said, "Michael, since you're our home evening dad, what advice would you have for someone like me?"

"I'm not a home evening dad. I'm a home evening group leader."

Alicia shrugged. "Whatever. Here's my problem. I've been here for almost a year, and so far I haven't had a single date."

"I'm sure that's probably typical."

"I know, but it's so frustrating."

"So what do you want me to do, give a lesson about how to change that?"

"That's not what I was thinking," Alicia said, "but, okay, sure, why not? You're smart. Will you teach us how we can date more while we're here?"

"Well, actually," I stammered, "basically, Heather and I just assign people to say prayers, things like that."

"I'd be interested in a lesson on dating," Benjamin, a senior in computer science, said. "I've tried to get dates, but the girls are always too busy."

"Looks like we're in agreement," Alicia said. "We'll have Michael give us a lesson next Monday."

"I'm sure Heather would do a better job than me," I said.

Heather shook her head. "I don't agree. Since I'm waiting for a missionary, I'm pretty much out of the loop for dating."

All through the week, whenever I saw someone on campus from our home evening group, they'd call out something like, "We're all looking forward to your lesson on Monday!"

On Thursday I called Heather. "I have no idea what to say on Monday. Can you help me?"

"You're so smart. I'm sure you'll come up with something worthwhile."

"I'm not their father. This is not part of my calling."

Nothing came to mind until Friday morning in one of my classes, and then, like a bolt of lightning, it all became very clear.

My teacher was talking about networking in my organizational practices class. Suddenly everything fell into place. I raised my hand.

"Yes, Michael," the teacher said.

"This will work in other areas! Thank you very much!"

After class, I ran to my apartment and within a couple of hours, I laid out the entire networking system for dating.

On Monday at home evening, I was very excited as I began my lesson. "Okay, what we're going to do tonight is called networking. It's used a lot in business."

I passed out five three-by-five cards to everyone. "Okay, what I want you to do is, on each of your cards, write down the name of someone you know on campus this semester. If you're a guy, write down the name of a girl, and vice versa. This could be a brother or sister, a cousin, a friend from high school, someone in one of your classes that you're friends with but have no interest in dating. I'll wait while you write down the names."

While everyone was busy, I talked with Heather. "How's Russ doing on his mission?" I asked.

"Real good. He's been made a zone leader."

"Good for him!" I always had a difficult time talking to Heather. My first tendency was to just stop talking, look at her, and say something stupid like, "Being around you takes my breath away." Of course I would never say anything like that. I'm in business management, for crying out loud, not poetry or art.

We were still maintaining eye contact.

"He's been gone sixteen months," she said. "Sometimes I can't even remember much about him." She sighed. "But it's support from friends like you that make me want to wait until he gets back."

"You'll do it, too. I'm sure of it."

She frowned. "Yeah, I suppose. Oh, Michael, in case I haven't told you, I really enjoy working with you."

"I enjoy working with you too. Thanks for being so on top of things. It's very seldom a girl your age is this organized. That means a lot to me."

She smiled. "Well, you're the organized one tonight."

"Thanks. I've even put this in a Power Point presentation."

She touched my arm. "I'd love to see it sometime. I love Power Point."

"Me too. It's very intuitive software."

"Intuition is good," she said. "Feelings are good too, don't you agree?"

"Yes, although sometimes I have a hard time admitting I have feelings for someone."

"I know you do, Michael, and, as a friend, I'll try to help you with that."

Suddenly, we noticed that everyone had quit talking and was staring at us. It was obvious that everyone was ready for the next step.

"Okay, then, is everybody done?" I asked. "The next step is for the guys to get in a circle on the floor, and the girls to get in another circle. Now, how this works is each of you take one of your cards and describe that person as best as you can. Then the next person does the same thing until you've all gone through all your cards. Are you with me so far?"

They nodded.

"Now as the names are being read, write down the ones you think you might want to go out with. Okay, you can go ahead with that."

While they were busy, I returned to Heather.

"You've given this a great deal of thought, haven't you?" she asked.

I nodded. "We were talking about networking in one of my classes, and all of a sudden I decided it could be adapted to dating."

"Well, so far, I'm very impressed."

Heather and I were, once again, looking deeply into each other's eyes. And then, almost as if on cue, our mouths opened slightly, and we slowly ran our tongue along our upper lip. Because it was such a strange thing to do, and because we'd done it almost in unison, we both blushed and turned away. To break the awkwardness, I blurted out, "So, does Russ enjoy being a zone leader?"

She moved a little farther away from me. "Yes, he does, very much."

We both gave a sigh of relief. We were back on safer ground now.

"Of course, it keeps him very busy," she said.

"I'm sure it does. I always appreciated the work of the zone leaders when I was on my mission."

"Did you work with zone leaders?"

I knew it was a cheap shot, and felt ashamed of myself, but I couldn't stop myself. "Well, yes, actually, I did. I was an assistant to the president."

She seemed impressed. "Really? I didn't know that."

"You probably think I said that just to impress you, don't you?"

"No, not at all."

"Good, because I don't care that much what you think." I cringed after saying it. "Sorry, that's not what I meant. What I was trying to say is that, well, since you're waiting for Russ to get back from his mission, there's no point in me trying to impress you."

She smiled. "And the way you're babbling now, you can rest assured you're not."

We both laughed.

By this time everyone was ready for the next step again. "Okay, here's the way this works," I announced. "Let's say one of the names on my list is my cousin Jill. Suppose that Troy here would like to go out with her. So he lets me know that, and then I call Jill up and say something like, 'Jill, my roommate Troy and I are planning a double date on Friday.' Then I'd tell her a few things about Troy, and end up with, 'If you'll go out with him, then I'll go out with one of your roommates, and we'll have a great time.' If she agrees, then we're good to go."

Everyone seemed to have strong feelings why this would fail horribly. I let them talk about it for a while, and then took charge. "Okay, people, listen up. This will work! I guarantee it. The question is, will you give it a shot?"

After some discussion, they all agreed to try it.

"Okay, then. If we all do this week after week, then I think that maybe after 20 or so times, one or two of us might actually meet someone we'd like to go out with again. But first you do the 20 iterations, okay? This is a statistical process based on probability, and the more times we do this, the greater the chance we'll find someone we match up well with. So we'll keep at it until the end of the semester."

"You're just trying to marry us off, aren't you, Michael?" one of the girls complained.

"No, not at all. The purpose of this isn't to get married. It's to meet more people and have a good time. Networking will work if you do it. Now, get together and figure out who's going to go out with whom."

Half an hour later everyone had a plan for the weekend and left to make their phone calls. Heather and I ended up sitting together on the couch.

"This is a really good idea," she said.

"Thanks, I hope it works."

"It should," she said with a sigh. "I haven't gone out with anyone for a long time. Sometimes I miss it."

I reached across her shoulders and gave her a quick hug. "Sure, but, you know what? It won't be long now, and then Russ will come home, and then all your waiting will pay off."

She sighed. "I suppose you're right."

On Saturday night at nine forty-five, I phoned Heather. "Have you had any feedback so far on how networking has gone?"

"The ones I've talked to who went out last night were very excited about what happened. A couple of girls said they're planning on going out with the same guy next week."

"Tell 'em they're not supposed to go out with the same guy. This is a statistical process. Everyone is supposed to start over again the next week."

"You'd better explain that at our next home evening."

And so, on Monday, I talked some more about networking. "People, don't even think about going out with the same person you went with last weekend."

"But what if I really like the guy?" one of the girls asked.

"You have to repeat the process over and over. Five, six, ten, twenty iterations. It's a statistical process."

"Well, I don't care what you say. We're going out again."

Two other girls said the same thing.

"If you insist on going to go out with the same guy, I want to meet him and make sure he's good enough for you."

"Michael, you're not their dad," Heather said.

"You think I don't know that? Well I do, Heather. I know that. But you know what? It doesn't matter! I still want to meet any guy that's dating one of my . . ." I paused, suddenly realizing how stupid it sounded. ". . . girls."

Heather leaned into me and patted me on the back. "Michael, it's great you care about us so much, but I really don't think approving who the girls in our group go out with is a part of our calling."

I thought about it for a moment, then said, "You're right. Let's move on. Who has the game tonight?"

After home evening, I asked Heather if I could walk her to her apartment. She readily agreed.

"This isn't going the way I thought it would."

"I know, but everyone seems happy about it."

I started to move my hand slowly in a large circle. "It's supposed to be first iteration, second iteration, third iteration, and so forth. It's a statistical process."

"I know but look on the bright side. Some of these girls haven't gone out for months, and now they are, thanks to you. That's got to give you some satisfaction."

"I suppose. It's just that . . ."

"What, Michael?"

I sighed. "I worry some of the girls are going to get their feelings hurt."

"That's the risk we take when we start pairing up, isn't it?"

"I guess so."

"You're not their dad, Michael."

"I know that, but still . . ."

"You really care about us, don't you?"

"Yeah, I do."

She leaned against me as we walked. "Can I tell you something? I used to think you were, well, I don't know how to say it, but, well, cold and mechanical and only interested in yourself. But now I see that isn't true. Now I see that, deep down, you're one of the nicest guys I've ever known."

I reached for her hand, and she didn't pull away.

We walked slowly, holding hands, enjoying each other's company.

At her door, I said, "I thought about holding your hand lots of times. I just never thought it would happen."

She smiled. "Why's that?"

"Well, besides the fact you're waiting for a missionary, I knew that if we paired up, it would set a bad example."

"In what way?"

"In terms of networking."

She moved away from me. "I'd better go in. I have some homework to do."

"Yeah, me too. I'm very busy this semester."

She seemed to be mad at me. "I think you've only said that about a hundred times! Are you that desperate for an excuse not to spend time with me?" She slammed the door on her way in.

At our next home evening, Alicia told us she and the guy she'd gone out with ten days before had shared a good night kiss and they now were talking about getting married.

I went ballistic. "Are you crazy? You only did one networking iteration, for crying out loud! How many times do I have to tell you people—this is a statistical process! You think this is like some cheesy movie where everyone gets married in the end? Well, it's not, okay? This is real life!"

"I know it's real life," Alicia shot back. "But sometimes real life is also the beginning of real love."

"Listen to me! Real life is where you drift from one person to another, and none of them is ever acceptable. Or else you find the perfect girl and she's waiting for a missionary. That's what real life is like. It's not that you meet someone and fall in love in a few days."

The rest of the semester was a complete disaster. One by one, every person in our home evening group got engaged. It was awful.

I'd had it with everyone. When summer term started, I moved to another apartment building so I'd be in another ward where I wouldn't know anyone. Even so, I spent the weekends going to wedding receptions of those who'd been in our family home evening group winter semester.

The first wedding reception I went to was that of Alicia and the first guy she'd networked. She threw her arms around me and kissed me on the cheek. "Thank you, Michael! I will always be grateful to you for teaching me about networking."

"Actually, what you did isn't networking."

"Well, I don't care what it was. I just know it worked for Alex and me, and that's all I care about."

Eventually, news about networking spread beyond my old ward's boundaries. Someone in our old group had written up instructions and, before long, it was being used in other home evening groups.

One day in my computer class, a girl approached me. "Michael, have you ever heard of networking, in terms of dating."

I shook my head. "No, I've never heard of it," I grumbled.

She explained it to me, and then said she'd go out with one of my roommates if I'd go out with her roommate.

"I'm not interested. I'm very busy this semester."

She playfully slugged me on the arm. "You remember when I gave you my notes for the day you missed class?"

"Yeah, so?"

"The way I look at it, it's pay-back time. You owe me this."

I sighed. "All right, I'll go out with your roommate."

I had so little interest that I didn't even ask about her roommate. And so I was very surprised when my roommate and I went to pick up the girls and found that Heather was to be my date. Heather, for crying out loud. I mean, what are the odds?

As my roommate drove us to the movie theater, Heather and I were in the back seat. I turned to her. "I can't believe it."

"Believe what?"

"Statistically speaking, what are the chances we'd randomly get set up?"

She laughed. "Actually, this is probably not as random as you might imagine."

"Really?" My heart began to race.

"Really."

"Well, it's supposed to be random."

"I guess we'll just have to make the best of it, right?"

"I guess so." There was one question that needed to be asked. "What about Russ?"

"He and I hardly know each other anymore. We've both changed so much. I sent him a Dear John letter about a month ago."

"How did you know it was time to break up with him?"

"I found myself thinking about another guy all the time. And that was even after I did some networking of my own. For me networking was one totally unacceptable guy after another. I'm so sick of it."

We were doing the eye contact thing again. I had forgotten the effect she had on me when I was with her. I swear I started to think about writing a song and dedicating it to her. For someone like me, that's not good.

"Networking is a statistical process," I said.

"I don't want a statistical process right now in my life."

I forced myself to break our gaze so I could think more rationally. "What do you want, Heather?"

She pursed her lips, not sure if she should say it or not. Finally she sighed, and said, "I want to spend all my time with just one guy."

"I'm ready to do that too."

"Really? I wouldn't expect that from you. I mean, after all, you're the king of networking."

"Are we talking about you and me seeing each other on an exclusive basis?"

She laughed. "An exclusive basis? You are such a romantic."

"You know what I mean."

"I think that's what we're talking about."

I grinned and yet shook my head. "This is awful."

"Why's that?"

"Everyone really is going to get married in the end, aren't they?"

"Maybe so, at least in our home evening group. We're the only ones left. So it might happen, if we play our three-by-five cards right."

"I've had it with three-by-five cards," I said.

She moved her hand slowly in a large circle. "No more first iteration, second iteration, third iteration? No more statistical process?"

"No, not anymore. Not for me."

"That's the way I feel too."

I smiled and reached for her hand.

Two months later, against all my predictions to the contrary, everyone (in our home evening group, that is), really did get married in the end.

When You're Here, You're Family

"Mandi, you know what? I don't think we kissed last night," Victor said as we made our way to my home in Cheyenne, Wyoming.

"I can't remember."

"We were about to kiss at the door, like usual, but then your roommate came out and said your dad was on the phone. So we missed out. That means we can kiss twice tonight."

It was times like this when I wasn't sure I'd done the right thing in getting engaged to Victor. He was a great guy and everything. Very smart. Faithful in the church. Taller than me, dark brown hair, good smile. He had a lot going for him. Sometimes, though, he reminded me of a dog begging for food at the table.

"Victor, I'm not sure we can store up unused kisses. I mean we never talked about that when we came up with our rules of engagement."

"But it makes sense we'd be able to save 'em up."

"Suppose you went away for a week. You wouldn't expect a week's worth of kisses when you came back, would you?"

"Well, yeah, I mean I'd have earned 'em."

"Let's change the subject, okay?"

"You're always saying I'm not spontaneous enough for you. What if I pull into a rest stop right now and collect my two kisses?"

"Victor?"

"Yes?"

"I'm not a vending machine. Give it a rest, okay?"

He thrust out his lower lip to let me know he was pouting. Oh please, don't let my future sons grow up to be like Victor, I thought to myself.

I'm twenty-two years old and teach high school P.E. in Salt Lake City. My hobbies are running marathons and kick-boxing.

Victor is my age and teaches English at the same school. We met at a two-day faculty retreat. Spending time together at the retreat was an escape from boredom. We even skipped one session to take a walk. I liked it that it was his idea to skip the session. I remember thinking, this is my kind of guy.

Unfortunately, since we've been engaged, we've missed very few meetings. Victor loves meetings. And agendas, and budgets, and Palm Pilots. Victor's dad died when he was six, so he was raised by his mom. Sometimes, like with the pouting, it shows.

I, on the other hand, was raised by my dad. My mom died of cancer when I was ten. It was like a part of me died with her. My dad took it pretty hard, too. He quit his job as a corporate lawyer in Salt Lake. We drove to Wyoming. Our plan was to stop at the first small town with a school, good scenery, and a lake nearby.

That town was Afton, Wyoming. My dad sold our home in Utah and bought a small house a few miles from town. For the first year he didn't work at all, but then because of some friends he made there, he became a guide, leading tourists with more money than common sense into the mountains. Because he couldn't leave me alone, he took me with him. And, so I wouldn't just sit around and whine, he hired me to help out. I loved the mountains and the freedom they gave me.

I suppose we'd still be there if my dad wasn't such a big mouth. When it came to issues about state government, my dad began asking questions. And the questions were so good that before we knew it, he'd been elected as Wyoming Attorney General. It meant that even though we kept our little house in Afton, we had to move to Cheyenne, the state capitol. We moved when I was fourteen. At first I didn't like it. I got in a few fights with some girls who thought they were better than me, and when my dad heard about it he got mad and told me I needed to learn to be more of a lady, which meant I took piano lessons.

He had a woman come in once a week and teach me proper manners. At first I fought the whole idea, but after a while I just decided to keep my wilderness guide self hidden, like my dad was doing, and try to fit in more. And I did. My love for physical activity was channeled into playing high school volleyball, basketball, and track. And so, when it came time to go to college, I picked physical education as my major.

In some ways, Victor, being raised by his mom, was raised almost as if he were a girl. His dad had been verbally abusive to Victor's mom, and died in a tragic car accident before she could move ahead with her plans to divorce him.

Victor had a knack for home decoration. He could walk in a room and immediately tell what was wrong with it. And most of the time, he'd do just that.

When Victor and I were on the same page, we were very good together. It's just that it hadn't happened much since we'd been engaged. He was needful of my affection and was constantly draping his arm around my shoulder or holding my hand. I was okay with that at times but sometimes I just wanted it to be how it was when we first met, us taking long walks and talking.

At any rate, we were on our way to visit my dad in Cheyenne. Victor's mom would be flying in from Sacramento that afternoon. Our original plans had called for us to pick his mom up at the Cheyenne airport, but we had some car problems and got a late start. I'd called and asked my dad to pick her up instead.

Which caused me just a little concern. My dad was not an easy man to get along with. His natural tendency was to be bull-headed, opinionated, and argumentative. I wondered if Victor's mom would be in tears by the time we made it to Cheyenne.

We were on I-80 in Victor's Honda Civic and he was driving at the speed limit, which drove me crazy. I desperately wanted to get there a little faster.

"Victor, you look tired. Why don't you let me drive so you can take a nap?"

"I'm not tired."

"Well, to me you look tired. I want you to be alert and wide awake when you meet my dad. Besides, I know this road like the back of my hand."

He yawned and pulled over, and a few minutes later, after he fell asleep, we were going ninety miles an hour.

Half an hour later we got pulled over.

Victor woke up as I was slowing down.

"Why are we stopping in the middle of nowhere?" he asked.

Before I could answer, a state cop was outside my door asking me for my driver's license.

"Is something wrong, officer?" I asked.

"You were going ninety five. The speed limit is seventy five."

"Oh, I'm so sorry, officer. It's just that I was trying to get home to see my dad. He's not been feeling well lately. Oh, you know what, maybe you know him? He's the attorney general for Wyoming. He often talks about what a fine job you men do to promote safety."

"Your dad is the attorney general?"

"Yes, he is. Ordinarily I wouldn't speed, but he's been sick and asked me to come home. It's not life threatening, of course, probably just a little cold, but you know how it is." I sniffled. "I love him so much. I just don't know what I'd do . . ."

The officer handed back my license. "Tell your dad to get better real fast."

"Thank you so much, Officer. Have a good day."

We drove away.

"I am shocked, Mandi, just shocked."

"Of course you are, Victor. That's what I'd expect you to be."

"First of all, that you were speeding, and second, that you would bring up that your dad is attorney general, and third, that you would lie to get out of a ticket."

"Sorry, Victor."

Victor then lectured me. I hate it when he does that but I let him do it because he needed to do it. Why did he need to? Because we're engaged. If you don't know what it means to be engaged, let me tell you. Being engaged means the physical part of your relationship has a tendency to take over, which causes a great deal of tension because you both want to be married in the temple. You keep having to impose tighter rules the closer you get to the wedding date just to make sure you'll be worthy to be married in the temple.

That's where we were now. Except Victor was more needful than me. Much more needful.

It also means that there are times when you wonder if you did the right thing and if you'll actually be able to last an eternity with the guy you're engaged to. One of the times that happened for me was when Victor lectured me, like he was doing then.

The other times I had doubts about being engaged was when I was with his mom. I'd met her once before. Victor and I had driven down to stay with her over April Conference.

Her name is Clarice Elizabeth, and wouldn't you know it, she goes by both names. Don't you think that if you had a name like that, you'd pick one or the other, and go by just it? Not that I'm complaining. She has the right to have people call her whatever she wants.

Clarice Elizabeth is tall for a woman of her generation. She's maybe five foot eight. She hasn't put on any weight since college, or so she told me during conference weekend when I asked how she managed to look so healthy. She said, "I watch what I eat and try to exercise every day."

"Well, you look very good for someone your age."

Clarice Elizabeth had cleared her throat, like she didn't appreciate me mentioning her age. She has an annoying habit of clearing her throat when she's uncomfortable.

From the moment I met her, I was pretty sure she didn't think I was good enough for her precious Victor. Or that I was almost acceptable if I'd just make a few changes in my life.

Like, on April conference Sunday, when I walked into the kitchen fifteen minutes before conference began, wearing my sweats, she said, "Amanda, do you need to change attire before conference begins?"

I went out to the driveway and looked at Victor's car and then came back in. "No, everything's fine. What made you think I needed to change a tire?"

"Oh, I'm sorry. When I said change attire, I meant, do you need to change your clothes before conference begins?"

"Not really. This is what I usually wear when I watch conference."

She cleared her throat. "That's fine. It's just that Victor and I like to wear our Sunday attire for conference. We believe it helps us to be more in tune to the proceedings, so that we get more out of conference."

"Well, good for you," I said.

A long pause, another clearing of the throat. "You do what you think best, dear."

"I sure will." I should have just let it drop, but I didn't. "You know the General Authorities can't see what we're wearing when we watch Conference, don't you?"

"Yes, I know that."

"Good, I wasn't sure if you did or not."

Clarice Elizabeth cleared her throat again.

So I wasn't looking forward to my dad and Victor's mom getting together.

Of course I knew my dad was not an easy man to live with. He loved to argue politics. When he did go out with a woman, he would always find some political issue to argue about. He'd end up driving his point of view so hard that she'd start crying and ask to be taken home.

And so, I had concerns. Because of the car trouble which delayed our leaving, my dad and Victor's mom would be together for several hours before we joined up with them. Usually, my dad only needed an hour to cross-examine a woman until she broke down and cried.

"Victor, I'm a little worried about my dad and your mom together without us. I love my dad but, see, the thing is, he can come on a little strong sometimes. He's a man with strong convictions and he doesn't mind saying when he doesn't agree with someone. Your mom seems, well, a little stiff, and the combination might cause sparks right from the start."

"Relax, my mom can get along with anyone."

"Well, not everyone. I didn't feel that comfortable with her on conference weekend."

"That's just because you weren't used to her."

"That's just my point. My dad doesn't get used to people. They either accept him for what he is, or as he likes to say, 'It's my way or the highway.'"

Victor frowned. "My mom has said that to me a time or two."

"I'm a little worried."

"You want me to pull over so we can talk about it?"

I thought he was being noble. But after pulling over at the next rest stop, he said, "How about if we kiss a few times before we talk?"

"Just drive, Victor, okay?"

"Is this the way it's going to be when we're married?" he asked.

"You know what? I was just thinking the same thing."

Needless to say, there was a little tension in the car when we pulled into the quarter-of-a-mile-long gravel road leading to our house.

My dad and I lived about ten miles outside Cheyenne. It's an old house, built on ten acres of wooded area and sage brush. It's the kind of house a wilderness tour guide like my dad would want, far enough away from civilization so no neighbors are around to remind him that he'd given up the love of his life, living in the wilderness, for more money.

It was dusk when we slowly made our way up the road to the house. Just as it came into view, out of the corner of my eye I saw my dad with a gun in his hand, chasing a woman. They ran into the trees.

"Did you see that?" I yelled.

"See what?"

"I just saw my dad chasing your mom with a rifle in his hand!"

"Seriously, what did you see?"

"Stop the car! We've got to find them before my dad does something he'll regret for the rest of his life."

He stopped the car and we both got out. "I didn't see anything."

"I know you didn't, Victor. But I did. And this is one of those times when you're going to have to trust me. They went this way. C'mon, let's see if we can find them."

We had only taken a few steps when we heard a shot ring out.

"Oh, no! He just shot her!" I cried.

Victor was not taking any of this seriously. "Look on the bright side, maybe he missed," he joked.

"My dad doesn't miss! If he shoots, he hits his target. The shot came from over there. Let's find them and see how bad she's hurt."

Victor started laughing. "Yeah, right!"

Another shot rang out. I knew it meant he'd only wounded her on the first shot and was now putting her out of her misery. He was very compassionate that way.

"What do you think is happening now?" Victor asked with a big smile on his face.

I wanted to shelter Victor for a few minutes. "It doesn't mean anything. Let's just keep looking."

I felt bad for him and wanted to spare him the pain of seeing his mom dead with two bullets through her, and my dad sitting on a rock enjoying the feeling of accomplishment that comes at the end of a hunt. I could only think of one thing to do. I turned around. "Victor, kiss me!"

"What?"

I put out both hands like I was a traffic cop trying to get a car moving toward me. "Here I am, Victor. Free kisses! Help yourself to as many as you want."

Victor looked around. "What about our folks?"

"Oh, there will be time enough to deal with that situation later on."

"Well, okay, maybe just a few, and then we'll continue to look for our folks."

We were about to kiss when we heard two people laughing. They were coming our way. I grabbed Victor and pulled him down behind some trees so we'd be out of sight.

We watched in shock as my dad and his mom walked past us. My dad had his arm draped around Victor's mom's shoulders, and they were laughing.

Just as they passed us, I stood up. "Dad, what's going on?"

Looking like two deer caught in the light of an oncoming car, they turned to face us. It was then I realized they were both carrying rifles.

"Mom? What were you two doing in the woods?" Victor asked.

"Paint-ball wars!" she said with a low deep laugh. "And I nailed him twice! Isn't that great?"

"She did! She got me twice! Great instincts for the first time!"

They high-fived each other.

I noticed Clarice Elizabeth was wearing a pair of my jeans and one of my old sweatshirts. I'm not sure what made me the most upset about it, that, at her age, she could get into my clothes, or that she wasn't in her usual boring wardrobe. What's going on? I thought.

"Mom?" Victor said. "Is it really a good thing for you to be running through the woods in your condition? You know what the doctor said."

"The doctor is an idiot," she said with a big grin for my dad.

I knew where that had come from. I'd heard it from my dad after my mom died. We'd had every doctor we could think of trying to keep my mom alive, but in the end they didn't do anything for her. So after that, whenever anyone mentioned doctors, my dad said they were all idiots.

"But what about your feet?"

"It's not my feet. It's my shoes," she said. "I feel great in these!"

That's when I noticed what she had on. "You're wearing my boots?"

"I am, and they are so comfortable! I hope you don't mind."

I sighed. I was beginning to feel like my world was being turned upside down.

"Okay, Clarey Berry, let's go see what's in the house to eat."

Victor looked at me like someone had slugged him in the stomach. Apparently he'd never thought of his mom as Clarey Berry.

As we all made our way back to the house, Victor and I were not all that comfortable that my dad had his arm around Victor's mom's waist.

Inside the house, my dad and Clarey Berry insisted they cook the meal.

I took Victor to my room and we closed the door so we could talk. We sat down on the bed next to each other.

"I feel sick to my stomach," I said.

"I know. I do too. And, let me say, I don't really like it one bit that your dad is hitting on my mom."

"It takes two, Victor. Don't tell me you can't see how your mom is leading him on. I mean, she has her hand on his arm all the time."

"Who was it that put his arm around my mom when she quite innocently went to the refrigerator to see if we had any lettuce?"

"Your mom innocent? Don't give me that. What about her going, 'Oh, it's so hot in here. I think I'll take off my sweatshirt."

"It was hot in the kitchen."

"Oh, my gosh, Victor, are you that naive?"

It must have occurred to Victor where we were. "We shouldn't be here. Remember our rule about never being in a bedroom together."

"Oh, and I suppose you think I lured you in here? Is that what you think, Victor? I mean, it's not hard for you to think my dad is hitting on your mom, so maybe it runs in the family, right? Maybe I'm trying to make a move on you, too, right? Is that what you think?"

"No, I don't think that. To tell you the truth, at the present time, with my mom and your dad totally out of control in the kitchen, I have more important things to worry about than whether or not you'll dole out to me one of your pathetically anemic kisses."

"Anemic kisses are they? Well, I think I can spare you the agony of suffering through any more of them! Just go, Victor, okay? I have a really bad headache."

"Oh, and I suppose you think I don't?"

I saw him to the door, then went through my closet trying to find out what else of mine That Woman had borrowed.

Five minutes later there was a knock at my door. It was Victor. "Please let me in, Mandi."

"What for?"

"It's far worse than we ever imagined."

"How can you be sure?"

"I just saw them kissing in the kitchen."

I opened the door and let him in.

"That's not possible, Victor. You just said that so I'd let you in."

"No, it's true."

"What kind of a kiss was it?"

"It was a kiss on the cheek."

"It was your mom, wasn't it? She was the one who did it, wasn't she?"

Victor sighed. I felt so sorry for him. "Yes, it's true. She kissed your dad on the cheek."

"She's a brazen hussy then, isn't she?"

Victor looked like he was going to cry. "I've never seen her like this before."

Victor and I weren't hungry, but we knew we had to show up for dinner if only to keep our parents in line. It was like trying to stop a freight train.

"Clarey Berry, would you like some more elk steak?" my dad asked.

"Pile it on, Big Guy!"

Victor grimaced and turned to me. "This is elk meat?"

"Yeah, so?"

"Did your dad kill the elk we're eating now?"

I shrugged. "Either my dad or me."

Victor put his hand to his stomach and looked like he was going to throw up.

"Get over it, Victor. We've got more important things to worry about."

He leaned over and whispered in my ear. "I can't believe my mom is letting your dad call her Clarey Berry."

"Hey, you two love birds," my dad said, "you care to include us in your conversation?"

My dad was making a complete fool out of himself. It was time to pull out my biggest weapon against any woman trying to win a place in my dad's heart. That weapon was politics.

"Dad, Victor's mom believes the federal government should impose tougher gun control laws. As one who is a member of the National Rifle Association, and someone who is a strong advocate for the constitutionally guaranteed right to bear arms, how do you feel about that?"

It was like waving red meat in front of a lion. I had already won. I wondered if there was another flight out of Cheyenne that Victor's mom could be on that night.

The only problem was Victor's mom didn't break down and start crying and run out of the room.

She wouldn't back down. It was like watching a tennis match as each one countered the other's argument.

Five minutes later, Clarey Berry made an excellent point. "David, that is not true, and you know it! The Constitution does not, nor has it ever, guaranteed citizens the right to own any kind of weapon they might choose! I can't see why banning assault rifles or rocket propelled grenades is going to cause us to give up our way of government."

My dad, instead of answering her argument, suddenly broke into a big smile. "My gosh, Clarey Berry, isn't this fun? You're good at this, you know that?"

"Well, you're the champ, that's for sure. I haven't had to focus my mind like this since I was on the debate team in high school."

My dad patted her on the back. "You haven't forgotten a thing. If you lived here, I'd want you to come with me when we visit town meetings. You and me, we'd be the old one-two punch."

Our folks went into the kitchen to whip up a dessert for us.

"Oh, my gosh, Victor, I am so sorry," I whispered.

"What just happened?"

"Let me just say it's not good. My dad has never backed down from any debate, and he's never acknowledged his opponent was as good as he was. This is not good."

I had only one weapon left, and I played it after dinner when we were sitting in the living room. We have an elk head mounted on the wall, and my dad was explaining how he came to shoot the animal. Once again Victor looked like he was going to throw up.

I went in my room and brought out a scrapbook. A minute later I handed it to Victor's mom. "I have a scrapbook here of my mom. I thought maybe you'd like to go through it. It has a lot of pictures of my mom and dad when they were dating."

Victor broke into a huge grin.

"Thank you so much. I would like to know as much as I can about your mom."

To tell you the truth, I wasn't expecting that. I also wasn't expecting my dad to go through the scrapbook with her.

"She was absolutely beautiful," Victor's mom said as my dad showed her their wedding picture.

"She was." He turned the page for her. "We went to Yellowstone Park for our honeymoon."

"Paul and I went there too. Where did you stay?"

"Old Faithful Lodge."

"We stayed there too!"

"What year?"

Over the next minute or two, they discovered they'd stayed in the same room exactly one day apart. In fact, they figured out they might have even crossed paths in the lobby.

"I remember we had to wait for them to clean up the room after you two were done with it," my dad said.

"What a coincidence!" Victor's mom said. "I've always said that if I ever remarried, I would want to go back there."

"I've thought the same thing!"

Victor planted an elbow on the arm of his chair and propped up his head with his hands. It was a gesture of resignation.

Our parents insisted on cleaning up the kitchen. Victor and I went to my bedroom and closed the door. I had a raging headache and lay down, while he paced.

"Victor," I complained, "we have a serious problem."

"I know."

"It's much worse than you think."

He sat down on the bed and held my hand. "Are you sure it's okay if I'm in here with you?"

"Victor, I have no desire to share any kind of intimacy with you at this time. In fact, and this is really a strange thing to say, but as my dad and your mom get closer, it's almost as if you're becoming my brother."

"That's not good, is it?"

"No, it is not good."

"Is it okay if I lie down next to you on the bed?" he asked.

"I don't care what you do, Victor. Just don't touch me."

He lay down next to me, but then he tried to hold my hand.

I sat up. "What did I just say to you?"

"No touching."

"That's right. No touching."

"Sorry." He moved a few inches away from me. We were now both staring at the ceiling like two corpses in a morgue waiting autopsies.

"Victor, your mom and my dad are going to get married in the very near future."

"They are?"

"Yes, they are."

"How do you know that?"

"A woman knows things like this. You'll just have to accept my word. That's bad, of course, but it gets worse."

Victor stood up and started pacing again. "It gets worse? What could be worse than having a step-dad who kills innocent animals, a man who is argumentative and bull-headed, and a man who has absolutely no respect for me. How could it get worse than that?"

"If you'll quit whining, I will tell you," I said.

"All right, but I wasn't whining."

"Suppose my dad and your mom get married before you and I do. Then you and I will become brother and sister."

"But we'll never be brother and sister, in terms of bloodlines."

I sat up. "Picture the announcement of our wedding. It will read, 'Mr. and Mrs. David Baxter proudly announce the wedding of their daughter Amanda to their son Victor.'" I got up and began pacing. "Do you want to know who will come to our reception, Victor? Well then, I will tell you. Reporters from The National Inquirer, that's who! Our reception will be a freak show! Is that what you want, Victor? Or should I say, Brother?"

Suddenly Victor did get sick and ran for the bathroom. The sad thing was I didn't care. The way I felt I wouldn't have cared if I never saw him again.

When he was finished he came in and lay down on the bed.

Okay, I admit I felt sorry for him. I put a blanket over him. He rested for a few minutes and then slowly got to his feet. He looked awful. "Before I go to my room, could we kiss?"

I grimaced. "I don't think so."

"Why not?"

"Well, for one reason, you just threw up."

"I washed out my mouth real good."

"And, for another reason, I feel differently about you now. It's hard to explain. It's just that things are changing now."

I kicked him out of my room and went to bed.

At one-thirty there was a knock at my door. "Victor, for the last time, I'm not going to kiss you, so go to bed and quit bothering me!"

"It's not about that. Can I come in?"

"All right, come in."

He opened the door and stepped inside. Even though it was late, he was still dressed. "Your dad and my mom left to take a walk three hours ago. They haven't come back yet. I'm really worried."

"Why should you be worried? I know what's happening. Your mom is throwing herself at my dad. I'm the one who should be worried. Get out of here so I can get dressed. I'll meet you in the living room."

A few minutes later we were in the living room pacing the floor.

"Is there any chance they could have been attacked by a bear?" Victor asked.

"Quit trying to look on the bright side, okay? No, there's no chance of that. My dad can take care of himself—except when it comes to a woman doing everything she can to get herself married so she'll have it easy for the rest of her life."

"If there's anything like that going on, I'm sure it's your dad who's making it happen."

We paced and worried and took pot shots at the other's parent until two fifteen when they sheepishly walked in the front door.

"Do you two have any idea what time it is?" I yelled.

"If you just knew how worried we've been!" Victor complained. "And how upset Mandi has been by your thoughtlessness and disregard of us."

"We can explain," Victor's mom said.

Victor threw his hands in the air. "Go ahead and explain then, but, believe me, this had better be good!"

"It was such a nice night, and the moon was shining so bright, I talked your dad into taking me for a ride in his dune buggy."

"ATV," my dad said. "It stands for all-terrain vehicle."

She shrugged her shoulders. "Whatever."

"We ran out of gas and had to hike back," he said.

"You expect us to believe that?" I asked. "You never run out of gas. You always tell me to fill up before I go out."

"Well, this time I forgot."

"What really happened?"

They looked at each other. "We might as well tell them," Victor's mom said.

"We've been talking about getting married someday," my dad said.

"Well, that's just great!" I yelled sarcastically. "As if Victor and I didn't have enough problems! Now you drop this on us! Thanks a lot!"

Watching our parents making fools of themselves was too big of a strain for Victor and me. On Sunday night, just before Victor dropped me off at my apartment in Salt Lake City, I broke up with him.

Near the end of August, my dad and Victor's mom were married civilly in the Denver Temple.

I attended the wedding reception in Cheyenne. Victor and I stood in line and had to endure a lengthy explanation from our folks that we weren't really brother and sister, but, by then I didn't care if people thought we were. My feelings for Victor were different now that our parents were married to each other.

When school started in the fall, Victor didn't show up to teach. Nobody seemed to know where he was.

I didn't hear much from my dad, but didn't worry about it much because I knew he had to devote more of his energy to his new wife. She started sending me weekly e-mails about the family. I assumed she was also sending them to Victor, my new step-brother.

After a while I quit reading her e-mails.

On a snowy day in mid-November, when I returned home from work, I saw a four-wheel drive vehicle parked in the middle of the front yard of my apartment building. And what was even more unusual, the engine was running.

"What idiot did this?" I said to myself.

I opened the door and trudged up one flight of stairs. I was surprised to find the door of my apartment open. And I could catch in the hall the unmistakable smell of meat being grilled.

I reached in my purse and pulled out the hand-gun my dad gave me when I first moved to Utah to go to school.

As I entered my apartment, I saw a man in my kitchen. He was using a hunting knife to cut up lettuce.

I used the cop voice my dad had taught me when I was a kid. "Sir, put down the knife and step away from the lettuce!"

The intruder, sporting a beard, wearing jeans and a sleeveless coat, stepped away from the cutting board.

"What are you doing in my apartment?" I asked.

"Making you dinner."

"Who are you?"

"These days people call me Vic." He turned around and suddenly I realized who it was.

"Victor?"

"Not anymore. I'm a wilderness guide now. Your dad trained me. I can do anything he can do, but now, a little better."

I was having a hard time adjusting to this new Victor. His voice was the same, but he didn't look at all like the Victor I'd known.

"Who would hire you?"

"Anybody who hired your dad."

"What about teaching?"

"A wilderness guide is a teacher. He just doesn't have to put up with rowdy students. I may do this for the rest of my life."

"Why?"

"Why did your dad spend the last two months with me? Good question, considering he just got married. Why did he teach me everything he knew? Another good question. I think he does think of me, in some sense, as his son."

This was the final blow. Now I'd not only lost my dad, I'd lost the wilderness areas I'd grown up in. Now, instead of taking me hunting, my dad would take Victor, or Vic, or whatever he called himself these days.

"That's great," I said sarcastically. "But, look, you and your mom are on a roll, don't stop now. You want my bedroom in Cheyenne too? I'll move my stuff out the next time I go home."

"Quit whining, Mandi. I don't want your room. Are you hungry?"

"No."

"Don't give me that. Sit down and we'll eat."

"What are you cooking?"

"Elk. I shot it three days ago. When I was cutting up the steaks, it reminded me of you."

"That makes no sense."

"I know how much you love the outdoor life."

"I did, but now that my dad has you, I doubt he'll be wanting me to tag along with him."

"What if you and I worked together as guides? It works out better with two experienced guides."

"I already have a job," I said. "I teach school."

"So quit. We have a lot of business coming our way for the rest of the hunting season, and then, in the winter, we've got five or six bookings for cross-country wilderness skiing, so it's looking to be a good year. Just think about it, that's all I'm saying."

"All right, I'll think about it."

"Let's eat then."

Naturally I thought we'd eat at the kitchen table but he had other plans for us. He boxed up the food and drove us into the mountains and led me on a short walk through the trees to a place he'd prepared beforehand. He got a fire started, and we sat around the fire and ate and talked.

I'm not sure what it was that changed the way I thought about him while we sat there. Maybe it was the ease with which he did things outdoors. Or his self-confidence that was now a part of his personality. He was no longer needful of anyone, especially not me. I sensed that he knew he'd do okay regardless of whether I married him or not.

I noticed he'd set up a tent, which seemed strange if we were just going to eat. I wondered if maybe he'd set up sleeping bags and that he planned for us to spend the night. I reasoned that it would be okay if we were brother and sister, which he might now think we were, although his offer that I be his wilderness guide partner still wasn't clear in my mind. Did he mean that in terms of us being brother and sister, or some other way? I wasn't sure.

Somewhere between my first and second helping of pork and beans, I realized I was in love with Vic. I had all the old feelings that had made me love him as well as a cascading number of new reasons. And because I wasn't feeling like his sister, the existence of the tent posed new problems, and, we were, once again, back to staying temple worthy.

I decided I needed to face the issue head on. "I see you've set up a tent," I said.

"Yes, I did. It's brand new, and it has all the newest features. I just bought it."

"My dad has plenty of tents. So why buy a new one?"

"Because this could be our tent."

My worst suspicions were verified. Vic had it in mind for me to spend the night with him in his new tent. In changing from Victor to Vic, he'd lost his moral footing. I felt bad for him.

The only problem was that a part of me really wanted to be physically close to Vic. The truth is, at that moment, I wanted to kiss him until my lips got chapped.

"Of course we can't do that tonight," he said.

I gave a sigh of relief. "No, of course not."

"But, if we were married, we could spend our nights in the tent."

I slid next to him and wrapped my arms around him and whispered in his ear. "It seems like such a nice tent, Vic."

"Will you marry me and be my wilderness guide partner and sleep with me in the finest tent money can buy?"

"Yes, Vic, I will. And let me say this, the sooner the better."

"How about next Friday?"

"Well, I don't know. That seems a little rushed. I mean, we'd have to tell our folks."

"That's only one phone call now."

"Yes, it is. It's only one phone call."

We kissed twice and then he pulled away. "I think we'd better stop now."

"Yes, of course," I said quickly. I stood up and began pacing back and forth. "We'll only have to wait for a week, right?" I asked.

"That's right."

"Good. Let's go call our folks."

Vic pulled out his cell phone and made a call to my dad. Two minutes later they came roaring into camp on two brand new ATVs, gifts from them to us.

We had a great time as a family breaking in our ATVs, and, a week later, after being married in the temple, Vic and I enjoyed the new tent for the first time.

You're probably thinking I made him change to fit my image of what he should be, but that's not true. I still love the old Victor, and sometimes he surfaces. We're talking about going back to teaching again once we have our first kid. I will love him no matter what he becomes because I will always know that he was willing to change for me. That, to me, is the most important gift he could give me. And I will try to become whatever he needs me to be. That makes it a growing relationship.

Most of the time our relationship with each other is that of a husband and his wife, but once in a while, usually when we're with our folks doing things together, for a few minutes at a time, it's more like we are brother and sister.

Either way, though, it hardly matters. We love each other on a variety of levels and we couldn't be happier.

I guess it's like they say—families, whether they're newly made, like with Vic and me, or are spliced together, like with my dad and Vic's mom, can be and hopefully will be, forever.

What Can I Do for the Gerbil Today?

"And this is Melissa!" my mom said proudly.

I had no idea who Melissa was and why my folks had brought her to the airport to welcome me home from my mission. She didn't look like a cousin because in our family, we're born ugly. It's only after years that we get better looking. I was pretty sure this girl had been born beautiful and stayed that way. With her long brunette hair, brown eyes and cheerful smile, she was the kind of girl who got lots of Valentine cards in grade school.

"Welcome home, Elder!" she said enthusiastically. I thought we were going to shake hands, but without warning she gave me a hug. I backed away and looked to my mom for protection.

"It's okay, it's just Melissa," my mom said. Everyone seemed to think I knew what that meant.

"Hopefully she'll be part of our family once Robbie gets home," my dad said proudly.

"Little Robbie has a girlfriend?" I asked.

"I wrote you all about it, David," my mother said.

My mother's letters came every week. Unfortunately it took about that long to read them. Eight to ten pages made more difficult to read because my mother has terrible handwriting. So, the truth is, I didn't read every page.

"Oh, sure, of course, it's Melissa! Robbie's little friend!" I shook her hand vigorously. She wasn't little. In fact, she was only a couple of inches shorter than me, but I'd always associated everything with Robbie as being little.

"Melissa is staying with us this weekend," my mother said, "so she'll hear your talk in church and then head back to school."

"She's already part of our family," my dad said.

"What year in school are you, Melissa?" I asked.

"I'm a sophomore."

"What high school do you attend?"

She suppressed a grin. "Actually, I'm a sophomore at BYU-Idaho."

"It's the same college you went to before your mission," my dad said. "You remember, Ricks College? They changed the name while you were gone."

"You seem so young to be in college, Melissa."

"I'm twenty."

"So you're the same age as Little Robbie then, right?"

"Little Robbie is six-foot-four now," she said.

"I wrote you about that too," my mom said.

"Yes, of course you did."

Half an hour later we pulled into our driveway. I got out and stared at the house and gardens. It was like visiting an old friend.

After supper I met with our stake president and was officially released as a missionary. When I came home, I told my mom I was going to take a walk. "Do you mind if I tag along?" Melissa asked.

"No, not at all."

Everything in the neighborhood looked the same, except I knew it wasn't, because I wasn't the same.

"You didn't read all your mom's letters, did you?" Melissa asked.

"How did you know?"

"Robbie is having the same trouble. I'm filling him in on the things that are the most important. I could do the same for you."

"I'd like that."

"Okay, here are the highlights of the last two years. Your dog died. You aunt Sally got married while you were gone. Twice, actually."

"Twice?"

"A good man is hard to find."

"Apparently. You say the dog died. I didn't know we had a dog."

"Robbie got it after you left on your mission. It slept in your room."

"Well, that explains a lot. When I first went in my room, I was afraid the smell was from gym socks left under the bed for two years. Anything else I should know?"

"Your dad got downsized. He's now working as a sales representative for a software company."

"I had no idea."

"Don't worry. I'll help you through this."

"Thank you very much. You're very kind. Sorry I didn't know about you and Robbie."

"He's told me what a good influence you were on him. For that I thank you."

"Little Robbie . . ."

She shook her head. "Not anymore."

"Right. That's going to take a while to get used to. You like him a lot, don't you?"

"I do."

"If you don't mind me asking, why?"

"He's always been very considerate of me," she said.

"Really? I taught him that."

"How?" she asked.

"I gave him a gerbil for his birthday when we were in junior high. When I found out he wasn't taking good care of it, I took him aside and told him, 'Robbie, you've got to always be thinking, what can I do for the gerbil today? Think about the gerbil, not just once in a while, but all the time!'" I paused. "That's probably why he's so considerate of you."

"So that's why he put newspapers on my floor every morning," she said.

We both laughed. I was impressed because not too many girls I know did comedy.

"What did you call your gerbil?" she asked.

"We called it The Gerbil."

She laughed. "I see. Very creative."

"It was probably Robbie's idea."

"No, somehow, I think it was yours. You're funnier than he is. He's . . . well. . . ."

"Sincere?" I suggested.

"Yes, sincere. Very sincere."

We walked to a park to sit on the swings and watch the sunset. Or, to be more truthful, she watched the sunset, and I watched her. I used to beat my brother in nearly every game we played. So how'd he get so lucky to find her?

"We'd better get back," she said. "Your mom and dad will be wondering what happened to us."

"It's been great being with you. I mean, you being a girl, and all."

"You're very observant."

"I didn't think I'd be this comfortable with a girl right after my mission, but, with you, I am. I guess maybe it's because you're already a part of the family."

"I feel comfortable with you too, David."

We walked back, had family prayer with my folks, and that was my first day home.

My talk on Sunday went okay. In fact Melissa said it was good.

That fall at BYU-Idaho, I woke up every morning thinking, 'What can I do for Melissa today?' I wanted to do all I could to make her happy with our family so when Robbie got back, she'd want to marry him.

Since I had a car, I gave her a ride whenever she needed to go shopping. On her birthday, I took her a rose and told her it was from Robbie. I'm not sure she believed me.

When either of us needed a date, we called each other. Sometimes we lined up our roommates, but after a while we gave up and just hung out with each other.

At first we spent all our time talking about Robbie. She read me his letters to her and I told her what news my mother had received from him. We went over the pictures he sent us, and we talked about how much he was growing on his mission.

Gradually, though, Robbie became more of an abstract concept than a reality. I'd told her every Robbie story I could think of, and she had done the same with me.

Saying good night at her door became more complicated as time went on. At first it was easy. Just a quick "Well, I had a great time. Thank you very much. Good night."

But then there began to be long, awkward pauses at the door. One night we exchanged a hug. After that the hugs became a little longer. One night she asked, "You think we'll ever kiss each other?"

"I have been thinking about it."

"What did you decide?"

"I don't see how we can under the circumstances, do you?"

That made her mad. "What circumstances, David? It's not like I'm engaged to Robbie or anything. I'm also not his property he asked you to look after while he was gone."

"But the whole reason we see each other is because of Robbie."

"So . . . you wouldn't waste your time on me if it weren't for him, is that it?"

"He's my brother."

"You want to know the truth? Sometimes I can't remember anything about him. We talk about him all the time but sometimes it's like talking about the Easter Bunny."

"What do you want me to do?" I asked.

"I want you to go home, David! Right now! Good night!"

We stayed apart for nearly a week, but then we couldn't stand it any longer so we got back together, but we never again lingered at the door.

Tension grew between us as the months passed. We never talked about any feelings we might have had for each other because, well, that would have been very awkward.

Finally, the day arrived. Robbie was coming home. I picked her up after class and we started for home. Usually we had so much to talk about, but this time we were silent. "You must be very excited," I said.

"Yes, of course," she said in a dull monotone.

"Me too," I said. "I'm very excited, too." After a long pause, I added, "I'm very happy for you, too."

Her expression softened. "Thank you for being so kind to me."

I shrugged my shoulders. "I've been happy to help out."

"'What can I do for the gerbil today,' right? That's what this has all been about, hasn't it?"

"Something like that," I said.

"What will you be doing this summer?" she asked.

"I've been thinking of going to Alaska and working on a fishing boat. I think it'd be better for me to stay away this summer, what with Robbie being home."

She shook her head and turned away. "Yes, of course."

Two or three times we looked at each other, but I never could say what was in my heart. Neither could she.

Later that day, my folks, Melissa and I stood in the airport terminal as Robbie walked out of the jetway into our lives again. He hugged my mom and dad, then me, and then paused in front of Melissa and shook her hand.

"It's because he's still a missionary. He'll give you a hug after he's released," I whispered to her as we went to get Robbie's luggage.

On the way home, Robbie sat in the front seat while Melissa, my mom and I sat in the back.

"He looks good, doesn't he?" I asked Melissa.

"Yes, except he doesn't seem very happy I'm here."

"Give him some time to adjust."

My mom had spent more than a week preparing for the family dinner. We had all of Robbie's favorites. And then Robbie told us stories about his mission. At seven thirty he left to meet with our stake president so he could be released as a missionary. He returned at eight thirty.

"Now he can give you a hug," I said to Melissa when he returned. But that didn't happen. In fact, he paid very little attention to her. At nine thirty he excused himself and went to his room.

I followed him. "Do you remember the gerbil?" I asked.

"It's not still alive, is it?"

"No, it died. Do you remember what I always used to tell you about the gerbil?"

"Not really. I remember you were always after me about it, though."

"I told you to always ask yourself, 'What can I do for the gerbil today'?"

"And you're telling me this because?"

"Melissa is the gerbil in your life now, Robbie."

"She is?"

"Yes."

"Why?"

"Because she waited for you."

"When I first left on my mission, I used to worry she wouldn't wait. But then, near the last, I worried that she would."

"She did wait for you, though. So right now, you've got to think, 'What can I do for her today?' With the gerbil it wasn't that hard, but with Melissa it will be more difficult."

"You know what? I have no idea what you're talking about."

"My point is that right now she's all alone in the living room."

"Mom and Dad are there."

"Go in and pay some attention to her."

"I'm not sure I feel the same way about her now. It's been two years. We don't even know each other anymore. Besides, it's not like I owe her anything just because she waited for me."

"You do owe her something! You owe her going out and talking to her and trying to renew what you two had before you left."

"How about if in a week or two I give her a call or send her an e-mail?"

"How can you say that? Don't you care about her?"

"Actually, I'm not sure I do."

I slammed my fist on his desk. "You know what? It's a wonder the gerbil lived as long as it did!" I stormed out of the room and slammed the door, and saw Melissa there, probably wondering about my strange behavior.

"Can we take a walk?" she asked.

We walked for several blocks in silence. Then I said softly, "Robbie is really tired tonight, what with his flight and the different time zones."

"Robbie has a voice that just booms out, doesn't he? You can hear it even through a closed door."

It was then I realized she'd overheard Robbie and me. "I'm so sorry."

"I knew you would be. Can I ask you a question?"

"Yes."

"When you had the gerbil, even though it was Robbie's, did you ever look in on it just to make sure it had everything it needed, just in case Robbie had neglected taking care of it that day?"

"Yes, I had to do it. I couldn't leave it to chance."

"I knew you would do that." She paused. "So where does that leave us?"

"I'm not sure. What do you hope happens?"

"I'd be very happy if you were to continue to think, 'What can I do for Melissa today.'"

"You would?" I asked.

"Yes, and I'd love to do the same for you."

"Every day?" I asked.

"If you're willing."

"For how long?"

"Maybe for a very long time."

"Are we talking about the same thing?" I asked.

"I think we are. But before we go any further and end up embarrassing ourselves, I need to ask you a question. David, did you love the gerbil?"

I shook my head. "No, I just made sure it was okay."

She looked like she was going to cry.

"It was just a gerbil, okay?"

Finally it hit me we weren't talking about the gerbil. "Melissa, I love you very much and have from the first time I saw you."

"I love you too, David. You've gone from being Robbie's brother to my best friend and then . . . well, it's gone way beyond that."

We kissed for the first time.

"Would you like to have a gerbil someday?" I asked.

She shook her head. "How about a dog?"

"I'm allergic to dogs."

"A cat then?"

By the time we finished our walk, we'd decided on a gold fish.

A year later, I'm happy to report the goldfish is doing fine.

A Landmark Decision

Andy approached her after sacrament meeting. "You're back!" he said. Although usually out-going, he seemed to be holding back. She wondered if it was because he didn't want to be hurt again.

They made eye contact for a brief instant before she looked away, not wanting to encourage him. She nodded. "Just for a few days of course."

"It's good to see you. You cut your hair, didn't you? It looks good. Very professional. That's the look you're going for these days, isn't it?"

"Yes, that's right. You look good too." She meant it. He'd been tall and skinny in high school but now, at 24, he'd beefed up. Maybe from all the work he did as a carpenter. She had forgotten how sun-bleached his hair became in the summer, and how blue his eyes were.

"So, you're all done with law school?" he asked.

"Yes."

"That's good. I'm proud of you." He paused.

"Thank you."

"So, what happens next?"

"I've taken a job."

"Here in town?"

"No, in San Francisco. I start in September."

"Will you be here this summer?"

"No, I'll be moving to California to study for the bar exam."

"Oh, you can't study here?"

"I'll be taking a class about how to pass the bar exam."

He broke into a grin. "If the class had a final exam, it would be the bar-exam exam."

"Yes, I suppose it would."

"So, how long will you be in town?"

"I'll probably leave tomorrow."

"Stay one extra day. I have a graduation gift for you."

"You didn't need to do that."

"My gift takes a day to give you though. Do you want to know what it is?"

"I guess so."

"It's one perfect day. An entire day dedicated to you. You'll never have a better day. Satisfaction guaranteed."

"Can you give me the day back if I'm not completely satisfied?"

He smiled. "I'm working on that. C'mon, Emily, you deserve a break. You'll laugh, you'll experience thrills and chills, your body will be pampered and refreshed. And when it's over, you'll tell me it was the best day of your life."

In an instant the barriers between them seemed to melt away. She tapped his shoulder lightly. "This doesn't involve paint ball wars, does it? Like before we graduated? Me running through the woods and you chasing after me, hitting me with one paint ball after another. That, my friend, was not what I would call a perfect day."

"Hey, that was high school. I'm much more mature now."

It was his silly grin that always did her in. And his eyes. And so, against her better judgement, she agreed to stay an extra day.

That night she sat on her bed and went through a scrapbook from high school. Almost every picture was of her and Andy. They'd grown up in New Jersey. For most of their teen years they were two of only a handful of members of the Church in their high school.

For four years he came to her home for early morning seminary. Her mother taught the class. Because it began at six in the morning, she did not always get up in time to get ready. He'd seen her at her worst, her long dark-brown hair hanging like a messy mop, her eyes blood-shot, barely able to stay awake, but nothing seemed to matter to him. Each morning, no matter how bad she looked, he always called her Sunshine.

Even in high school they didn't seem to have much in common except for their membership in the Church. She was an excellent student and took A.P. English and A.P. History. He loved classes where he could use his hands, especially wood-working and auto shop. He became known in school for his skills in building and repairing. By his junior year everyone called him Handy Andy.

Because they were the only members of the Church in the same grade at their school, he took her to all the important dances. Near the end of their senior year, he told her he loved her.

She had not known how to respond. She didn't think of him that way. To her he was just someone who was always there for her.

That fall when she left for college, he enrolled in a trade school. After a year he began working full time as a carpenter.

At nineteen he left on his mission, faithfully writing her once a week. She answered only a few of his letters, not because she'd found someone else, but because she was so busy. She had chosen a fast-track undergraduate program, so by the time he returned she was, at twenty one, about to start law school.

A few months ago when she was home for the holidays, he asked her to marry him. She was embarrassed he didn't realize she felt she'd outgrown him. As politely as she could, she told him that although she valued him as a dear friend, she could never marry him.

Now he was offering her the best day of her life. She regretted having agreed to his offer. Not because it would be a waste of time, but because she was afraid she would end up hurting his feelings again.

Her perfect day began with her waking up at ten-thirty, even though she'd set her alarm. On her dresser she found a note which read, "Good morning, Sunshine! Come downstairs the way you are. Your perfect day is about to begin!"

When she entered the kitchen Andy was at the table talking with her mother. On the table was a large platter of fruit and breakfast rolls and a tall pitcher of orange juice.

"Look what Andy brought us," her mother said.

"I set the alarm for six fifteen."

"I asked your mom to sneak in and turn it off so you could sleep in."

"I was going to study for the bar exam."

"You can do that another day," he said. "Grab some food and we'll go."

"Go? Go where? I'm not dressed."

"It's a jogging outfit, Emily. Most people will just think you've been running."

She scowled at the tray of food. "I can't eat any of this."

"Why not?"

"I'm on a low-carb diet."

"Not today. On your perfect day, you can't be on a diet."

She was ready to call the whole thing off. "Andy?"

"What, Sunshine?"

She sighed. It's just *one day,* she thought. "Nothing, I guess." She placed some fruit and a muffin on a paper plate and poured herself some orange juice, taking a sip. It tasted wonderful. "Is this fresh?"

"I squeezed it myself," he said.

He drove her to a fitness club. "Are we going to work out?" she asked.

"No. I've arranged for you to have a full-body massage. You'll love it. Helga will give it to you. People around here call her Helga the Magnificent."

"Andy, how much is this costing?"

"On a perfect day, money doesn't matter."

The massage took an hour. Helga, in a mixture of English and Norwegian, talked the entire time, but most of the time Emily didn't understand what she was saying.

When Helga finished, she handed Emily some new clothes—cotton khaki slacks, a white cotton pullover, white socks, and a pair of the most comfortable shoes she'd ever worn. And a black eye patch.

When Emily stepped into the lobby of the fitness center, Andy was waiting for her. "Let's go," he said.

"What's the eye patch for?"

"You'll see. Let's go."

He drove her to the Delaware River where they boarded a boat. The pilot was a large balding man with a big belly and an infectious laugh who insisted they call him the Dreaded Pirate Roberts. He also insisted they put on their black eye patches and practice shouting, "Arggh!"

They ate lunch as they floated down the Delaware and listened to Pirate Roberts talk about the early history of the area.

After the boat trip they returned home. Andy gave her a drive-by tour of all the houses he'd built. They were expensive, featuring hand-crafted extras unavailable in tract houses.

The last one he showed her was more spectacular than any of the others. It was a large two-story brick house set on top of a hill overlooking the town. He pulled into the driveway and stopped. "I'm going to give you a tour of this place."

The home was finished, but vacant, and yet there was no "For sale" sign in front.

"You know how everyone puts an extra key under the welcome mat? Well, I've invented something better than that." He knelt down by the landscaped flowers near the front door and carefully slid open the top of what appeared to be a rock. He reached inside and grabbed a key.

He gave her a detailed tour, pointing out the features of each room.

Her voice echoed in the large, empty kitchen. "This is the most beautiful house I've ever seen. How long have you been working on it?"

"Three years. I started it when you began law school."

"Isn't that a long time to spend on one house?"

"I never planned on putting it on the market."

"Why not?"

"I built this for you, Sunshine."

She was stunned. "For me?"

"For us, actually."

She shook her head. "Andy, I thought we . . ."

"Don't say anything until the tour is over, okay?"

She followed him. "This will be the master bedroom," he said as they entered a cozy room with a bay window that overlooked the valley. "The closets are cedar and large, and there's one for each of us." He opened one of the closet's sliding doors. "Come here and take a whiff."

She did as he directed. "It smells very good."

He continued on to an adjoining room. "I'm not sure about one thing though for the bathroom. I need some advice."

The bathroom was unfinished. "Right there will be the bathtub and the shower. One possibility is to have three shower heads. Most people usually wash their front, turn around and wash their back. But with three shower heads, you wouldn't have to turn around. It's up to you, whatever you'd prefer."

She was near tears. "Andy, it makes no sense for you to be asking me that. I've already told you I have no intention of marrying you. This is too painful for both of us. I feel awful you've gone to all this work for nothing. Please take me home."

"Whatever you want, Emily, you know that."

She hated the tears running down her cheeks.

"Some bathroom this is, right? No tissues."

"If I ever said anything to cause you to believe we had a future together, I am very sorry."

He shook his head. "Oh, gosh, Emily, it wasn't you. It was me. This was just something to do after work, that's all. Sometimes I can't sleep at night, this helped me. Sure, I guess it's what people call living in a fantasy world, but that's okay. Don't worry about it. I always knew it was a long shot that we'd ever get married, but a guy can always hope, right?"

"Can we go now?"

"Before we leave, could you do me one last favor? Let's watch the sunset out this window. It's the last thing I'll ever ask you to do for me."

They sat cross-legged on a ledge in front of the bay window. They sat far from each other and looked straight ahead.

"You knew that after law school, I'd most likely never come back here to work. So why go to so much trouble?"

"I thought you might want to set up a law practice in town."

"So you just went ahead and planned out my life without even once asking me what I thought about it?"

"I can see why it might look that way to you."

"You've gone to all this work for nothing."

"That's not true. Have you ever had such a good dream that you felt bad when you woke up? Well, that's what this house has been for me. Upstairs is where the children's bedrooms would be. I even made up some wooden name plates to go on each of the doors. You just give me your favorite kid names and I could have the plates up in an hour."

"Andy, this is way beyond what would be considered normal. I'm really worried about you. You may need counseling to work through this."

He shook his head. "All I have to do is put the house up for sale, that's all. A guy like me don't need counseling."

"Doesn't need counseling."

He smiled. "I know. I just wanted to see if you'd correct my grammar like you did on my term papers in high school."

"What did you think I was going to do if I came back here?"

"I figured you'd be a lawyer."

"There's not enough work in this town to keep me busy. I'd never make enough money to pay rent on an office."

He didn't answer, making her suspicious. "Oh, no. You thought about that too, didn't you?"

"More or less."

She turned to confront him. "What did you do, Andy?"

"Truth is, I built a place in town for your office. Don't worry, though. I can always sell it. In fact, I've already had three offers."

"Why have you done this?"

"I've loved you since ninth grade, Emily. In fact, you're the only girl I've ever loved. Maybe the only girl I ever will love."

"I've got to get out of here," she said on her way out of the bedroom.

She waited for him outside.

"I need to put the key back," he said.

She watched as he returned the key to the rock. "Do you have anyone in your life right now?" he asked.

"No, I've been too busy for that."

"Maybe you'll have more time now. You know, it still might work out for us."

"I don't think of you that way."

"Maybe it's like . . ."

"Like what?"

"Maybe it's like . . . does a fish love the water it swims in?"

"I have no idea what that means. Please take me home."

A few minutes later he dropped her off. She told her parents what he had done.

"I'm not surprised," her mother said. "He's always loved you."

"We don't have the same goals in life."

"What are you most afraid of?" her dad asked. "That you'll end up happy?"

"You're both on his side, aren't you?"

She changed clothes and drove to the high school to jog around the track. She ran and walked for three hours before she felt calm enough to be able to sleep.

She woke up at two in the morning but she couldn't get back to sleep. She went in the backyard. There was a full moon.

I want to see the house one more time, she thought.

She put on some shoes and then stepped outside again. She didn't want her parents hearing her drive off and wonder what was going on so she ran in the moonlight to Andy's house on the hill. She retrieved the key and let herself in.

She made her way to the master bedroom and sat on the ledge in front of the bay window. There she had a silent conversation with herself as if she were questioning someone on the witness stand.

In your opinion, do you suppose you will ever have anyone in your life who will love you as much or more than Andy?

Probably not, but the fact is, I don't have the kind of love for him that would make me want to marry him.

But is it not true that in high school he was your best friend?

Yes, he was.

And is it not also true that whenever you had a problem or were discouraged or just needed a hug, he was always there for you.

Yes, that is true.

With all due respect, could not those attributes be considered a working definition of love?

Well, yes, I suppose it is love, but it isn't the kind of love between two people who want to get married.

That could change though, could it not? If given a chance.

Coming back here drawing up wills is not what I want to do with my life. That's not why I went to law school.

What do you want to do with your life?

I want to make a difference.

True or false—mothers make a difference in their children's lives?

You're badgering me, Counselor.

She walked slowly upstairs where Andy said he'd built children's bedrooms. There were five. She smiled at his optimism. As she passed each one, she tried to think of a name for a son or daughter.

In the last bedroom the moon was shining directly through the window. She sat down on the floor and watched it.

This is my last night in what could have been my home, she thought. *I'd like to spend the night here in this room.*

She ran home, grabbed a sleeping bag and a pillow, and ran back to the house. Once there, she headed for the last bedroom and got into her sleeping bag. A short five minutes later, she was asleep.

She woke the next morning to the sound of hammering in the front yard. She tiptoed downstairs, looked out the window and saw Andy pounding a "For Sale" sign into the ground.

She wanted to talk to him, but didn't want him to know she'd spent the night in the house. To cover it up, she ran out the back door, jogged into the woods, then circled back to the road just as he closed the tool box in the back of his pickup.

"I see you've got the house up for sale," she said.

"That's right."

"Actually, I might be interested in it."

"To buy?"

This was very hard for her to say. "Not exactly."

She could see the corners of his mouth begin to curve into a smile.

"It's too early to tell for sure right now if I'd be interested in the place, but I think it might be worth entering an investigative phase."

"I agree. An investigative phase is definitely what we need here."

"Oh, one shower head is all I'd want. I don't mind turning around when I take a shower."

"One shower head. Okay, I'll make a note of that."

"To be perfectly honest, it might take me a while to decide."

"Take all the time you need. Also, if you're in the market, I have a law office I could throw in. Hardwood floors, big windows, even a fireplace."

"Can we go look at it now?"

"Of course. Hop in."

She felt her face. It was hot to the touch. "There's one other thing. I have a little confession to make."

"What?"

"I . . . actually . . . slept in the house last night. That's breaking and entering. If you hire me as your attorney, I'm pretty sure I could put myself behind bars for a very long time."

"This is a serious case then, isn't it?"

"I'm afraid it is."

"Well, I will definitely want compensation."

"What are you asking?"

He snickered. "One more boat ride with the Dreaded Pirate Roberts."

"Arrgh!" she said, mimicking the boat captain.

"Yes, 'arrgh.'"

"I believe my client will accept those terms."

He went with her to retrieve her sleeping bag, then they locked up and got in his pickup.

As they backed down the driveway she scooted next to him and rested her head on his shoulder. She had forgotten what a good shoulder he had for things like that.

She smiled. It felt good to be back home.

The Best Way to Spend New Year's Eve

Christopher filled his plate in the kitchen and retreated to his room. His sister Kaitlyn, a high school senior, was having a party for her friends before going to the stake New Year's Eve dance.

He'd been back from his mission a little over a year. Living in Nebraska, there weren't many members of the Church in his age group. For that reason he had decided not to go to the dance. He'd stay in his room and play video games or get on the internet. His parents would also be going to the dance as chaperones.

He could hardly wait for everyone to leave. He liked being alone. He liked playing video games, and he liked surfing the web. Even so, knowing that he was going to be alone for several hours, he had a strange feeling. It was the feeling of walking along the top of a steep ice-covered roof, knowing that if he slipped it would be nearly impossible to keep from falling to the ground below.

"Not this time," he told himself. "I'm going to stay in control. I'm just going to play video games. I can stop this from happening again."

He turned on his computer and answered two messages from friends at BYU.

Someone knocked on his door, startling him. One of Kaitlyn's friends stuck her head in the room. She had a long narrow face with dark brown hair and a naturally tan complexion. She was wearing a Santa hat. "Sorry, I'm looking for the bathroom."

"This isn't it." He was relieved he hadn't been watching anything inappropriate, but at the same time embarrassed that he could have been.

"Why is your face so red?" she asked, coming closer. "You're blushing. Why? What are you doing in here?"

"Nothing. Who are you anyway?"

"I'm Hannah Banana Happy Piana."

"That's your name?"

"Not the Banana Happy Piana part, but my first name is Hannah. I'm a cheerleader."

"I can believe it. Well, it's always nice to meet one of my sister's little friends," he said with a tinge of sarcasm in his voice. "The bathroom is down the hall."

She looked around his room. "So, is this how you're going to spend New Year's Eve? Alone in your room? Aren't you going to the dance?"

"No."

"How come?"

"I don't like to dance, and none of my friends that I graduated with are still around. I wouldn't know anybody there."

"You know me, and I'll be there."

"You're the same age as Kaitlyn."

"So?"

"No offense, but I'd rather stay home than dance with one of her little friends."

"Stay home and what? Watch digital images? Do you know what a digital image is? I just learned about it. It's made up of a series of one's and zero's. That's preferable to talking to me?"

"You want my honest opinion?"

She mussed his hair with a swipe of her hand. "Can a digital image do that?" Next she slugged him on the shoulder. "Can a bunch of one's and zero's do that? Look at it this way. I may be too young for you now, but in nine months I'll be at BYU."

"So?"

"So at BYU, you won't be able to tell me apart from someone your age."

"I will once you open your mouth."

"Good job, you got me back good. Way to go. So come to the dance with us. Look, I'll teach you how to dance. I'll teach you how to carry on a conversation. I'll teach you not to be such a dead head all the time."

"What makes you think I can't dance or carry on a conversation."

"Kaitlyn told me. She also said you're a video game geek, and you scare girls away because you don't know how to talk to them."

"That's not true."

"I say it is. I say you're totally hopeless. Anyone can see that."

"Look, cheerleaders are not known for their great intellect. I really doubt you could teach me anything."

"I could teach you that staying in your room entertaining digital images when you could go to a dance is dumb. Especially when you could dance with me."

"Thanks, but no thanks."

She mussed his hair again. "Just think about it, okay? We won't be going for a few more minutes, so you can still change your mind." With that, she was gone.

He was glad to get rid of her and could hardly wait for everyone to be gone so he could be alone. At the same time, though, he dreaded what he might do after they left.

The truth was, it was hard for him to stay away from certain web sites. It had first happened at school when he was alone and started using his roommate's computer. At first just out of curiosity he had gone to a pornographic site. What he saw there was both disgusting and degrading. Even so, a few days later he went back. As time went on, he found himself returning again and again, until it was almost as if he had no ability to stop himself.

More than once he had promised himself he would never look at those sites again. Sometimes he went a day or two, but eventually he found himself back there.

After church on his last Sunday at BYU, he had gone somewhere to be alone. He'd closed his eyes and prayed. "Please help me stop doing what I've been doing." He had poured out his heart to God for help, but nothing seemed to change. And now he was home, and everyone was about to leave for the dance, and he'd be alone again. He both feared and looked forward to what would happen then.

He closed his eyes once more. "Father in Heaven, please help me. I can't start the new year doing what I've been doing. I have to change my life for good. Please help me to be strong."

He had no sooner whispered the words when the door flew open, and there was Hannah. "I'm here!"

His mouth dropped open. "What?"

"I'm here for you to take me to the dance where we'll dance the night away. You'll dance every dance, not just with me, but with all of Kaitlyn's friends."

She had a bell on her Santa hat and she was doing some kind of a dance for his benefit. The bell jingled and jangled throughout the house.

He stared at her and wondered if she could possibly be God's answer to his prayers. One thing for sure. He knew what would happen if he stayed at home. The only unknown was what would happen if he went to the dance.

He stood up. "Give me a minute. I'll need to change my clothes."

"He's going! I won the bet, Kaitlyn!"

A few minutes later he walked into the living room where six girls waited for him. "All right, let's light this candle!" Hannah shouted.

He ended up riding in the back seat while Kaitlyn drove. Two girls were crunched together on his left and two were on the right. Hannah chose the front seat.

She turned around to face him. "Christopher, what's your favorite color?"

"I don't know."

"Come on, you've got to pick one."

"Why?"

"It's one of the first things I learn about somebody when I meet them. You can learn a lot about a person if you know their favorite color."

"What can you learn?"

She undid her seat belt and leaned closer. In a secretive voice she whispered, "For one thing, you'll know their favorite color!" She slapped the back of the seat, laughing hysterically, then turned around and fastened her seat belt again.

"High school humor?" Christopher asked the girl on his left.

"I guess so. My name is Sarah."

Hannah turned around again. "Sarah, Bavaria, So Very-ah Cool! Yeah! Let's hear it for Sarah!"

Christopher's ears were ringing.

"Okay, you've had enough time, Christopher. What's your favorite color?"

"Blue."

"Why blue?"

"Because the sky is blue."

"Great answer! Good job! Blue is a good color. My favorite color is orange. I don't know why, but it just makes me happy. My bedroom is painted orange. Sometimes I wake up and pretend I'm living inside a pumpkin, like I'm one of the seeds."

"Maybe you're not one of the seeds," he teased. "Maybe you're that pumpkin slime you have to pull out with your fingers before you carve a pumpkin for Halloween."

"Pumpkin slime? Oh, gross! I hope I'm not that!"

The dance seemed to have been frozen in time until Hannah showed up with all her friends, and with Christopher in the middle of them all.

"We're here everybody! Let's party!" Hannah called out. She grabbed Christopher's hand. "I get the first dance because I got you to come.

They went out on the dance floor and waited for the next song to begin. "So you won a bet getting me to come tonight?" he asked.

"I did. I won a candy bar!"

He couldn't help but notice that when she smiled, a dimple magically appeared on her right cheek. "Where is it? I should get a part of it."

"You will, I promise. As soon as your sister pays up."

The music began.

He shuffled his feet.

"Okay, Christopher, start dancing," Hannah said.

"I am dancing."

She turned to her friends. "He thinks he's dancing!"

They all laughed.

"Do I have to teach you? Watch carefully: This is how you dance."

He watched her totally unpredictable and random movements, utterly confused.

"You got it?"

"Got what?"

"I can't believe you're older than me. You don't know much about anything, do you?"

"Actually, I'm very smart."

"Really? Well when we get to something you're smart at, be sure and tell me, okay?"

"Okay." He tried his best to copy her, but it was too hard.

She turned around. "Just do what I do, okay?" He followed her around the dance floor twice before she turned to face him again. "Okay, let's dazzle the crowd!"

They put on a show for his sister and her friends, who cheered enthusiastically.

"Okay, now dance with Melissa. Melissa, you're on! Don't undo what it's taken me so long to accomplish. You got ten minutes, then it's Sarah's turn."

Dancing with Melissa was okay but she wasn't as spontaneous as Hannah, so within a few minutes neither one of them were saying anything.

"Time out!" Hannah shouted. She ran over to them. "Melissa, I need to talk to Christopher for a minute, but I'll get him back to you soon."

Melissa returned to her friends on the sidelines.

Hannah grabbed his ear. "Let's take a trip to the hall, Buster! You're in big trouble."

On the way she tried to come up with a nick-name for him. "Christopher, Christopher, the mystery mister, should've met his true love, but instead he missed her."

Once they were a few feet down the hall she mussed his hair. "What were you thinking of back there with Melissa?"

"I was dancing the way you showed me."

"Why didn't you talk to her? What is wrong with you, anyway? You just stood there like a tall, silent, dancing Twinkie."

He scowled. "A dancing Twinkie? Where do you come up with this stuff?"

"Okay, I'll be Melissa, and you be you. Okay, talk to me."

"Don't you think that Hannah is the strangest girl you've ever met?" he asked.

Hannah wasn't amused. "Oh man, that is so funny. I'm cracking up here, Christopher. You're killing me with your humor."

Then she punched him lightly on the shoulder. "Get serious. We don't have much time, and there's so much to do. Okay, now you be Melissa and I'll be you."

He shook his head. "It's easy to be Melissa. All I need to do is stare at the floor and not say anything."

"Melissa, how many brothers and sisters do you have?"

"Four brothers, two sisters," Christopher said in his highest voice.

"And what are their names?"

"Winken, Blinken, and Nod, Donner, Comet, and Blitzen."

"Are you the oldest or the youngest?"

"I'm right in the middle."

"Do you have any hobbies, Melissa?" she asked.

"Yes," he squeaked. "I collect boilers from condemned high schools."

Hannah tried her best not to laugh. "How interesting."

"I keep them in my room."

"Must be a big bedroom."

"Yes, but it's always warm."

Hannah's resolve collapsed. They both laughed until their sides ached. They ended up sitting down, their legs extended and their backs against opposite walls of the hallway.

Hannah said, "Do you see how easy it is to carry on a conversation with a girl? You just keep asking questions about her life. But the trick is to be interested in the answers she gives. Okay, let's go back in there and see how you do."

For the rest of the evening, Hannah let him practice what she'd taught him. He danced with Hannah and all her friends in turn. A couple of times he even danced with his sister.

Hannah danced with him just before twelve. "Are you going to kiss us all at the stroke of midnight?" she asked loud enough for the other girls to hear.

"Count me out!" Kaitlyn cried.

"I don't know," he said. "What do you think?"

"I think it'd be okay if it was on the cheek. But the rule is you have to kiss us all within one minute after the stroke of midnight. Anything after that is not allowed."

"Where do you come up with these rules?"

"It's a gift," she teased.

As the countdown started, the girls huddled next to him, with the exception of his sister. The clock struck, and Hannah began counting. "One thousand one, one thousand two."

Melissa let him kiss her on the cheek.

"Hurry it up, folks! Time's a wasting!" Hannah called out.

Everyone was watching them. He kissed Sarah. The other two girls started laughing and ran away, leaving only Hannah counting.

"Only ten seconds left!" she called out.

He ceremoniously kissed her on the cheek and gave her a hug.

"All right! Happy New Year!" she yelled.

"Happy New Year!" he answered.

An hour later Kaitlyn drove him home and then drove her friends home.

Her parents had watched with delight as Christopher came alive at the dance. "You certainly looked like you had a good time tonight," his dad said.

"I did. I had a great time!"

"Thanks for making it so fun for Kaitlyn and her friends," his mother said.

They went in the TV room and watched other cities around the world celebrate the new year until Kaitlyn came home. She seemed happy to see Christopher. "Thanks for being such a good sport," she said.

"I had fun."

"I didn't think Hannah would get you to go."

"She's hard to turn down."

"She is fun, isn't she?" Kaitlyn said. "I think she might even like you."

"I like her too, but she's too young."

"She'll be at the Y next fall, so you never know."

After family prayer and good-night hugs, Christopher entered his room.

There was his computer on his desk, just waiting to be turned on.

Maybe I should check to see if I have any e-mails, he thought.

He sat on his bed and tried to decide what to do. In the past, something as innocent as checking his e-mail had eventually led to the internet and then to problems.

He felt that Hannah had been an answer to prayer, but she couldn't be with him all the time. How was he going to make it through the rest of the night? And what about the next day, and the day after that? Wasn't it inevitable that sooner or later he would return to the web sites that had been his downfall in the past?

He knelt by the side of his bed. "Heavenly Father, please help me stop this terrible habit before it takes over my life." *What else should I say?* He kept his eyes closed and tried to think how he could overcome his problem with pornography. Out of nowhere he heard Hannah. "What's your favorite color?"

The thought of asking one of the girls on a pornographic site a question like that made him smile. Those girls wouldn't answer such a question, and he wouldn't ask it of them. They lived in a one-dimensional world where only one thing mattered. One thing that promised everything, but gave back nothing of any lasting worth.

He went to his desk and began to write in his journal. "From now on I will spend my time with real girls, not virtual images on a monitor. I'll ask them what their favorite color is. I'll ask how many brothers and sisters they have. I'll ask them what their hobbies are. I'll dance with them, joke with them, tease and get teased by them, and I'll laugh with them. I will stay away from virtual girls for the rest of my life."

He signed it, looked up, glared at his computer, and hauled everything out to the kitchen.

He set up his computer there, where anybody coming into the room could see what was on the monitor.

His dad heard him moving about and came in. "What are you doing?"

"I'm getting ready for the new year."

"You're moving your computer into the kitchen? What for?"

"Dad, do you have a few minutes? There's something we need to talk about. Something I need to tell you. Something I'm going to need some help with."

They sat down and he told his dad everything.

When he finished, his dad suggested he work with his bishop when he returned to campus. Christopher agreed to do it.

"One other thing," his dad suggested. "Once your bishop feels you're worthy to go to the temple, I'd suggest you plan to go once a week. Being in the temple can help you stay strong."

Back in his room, Christopher looked around. It seemed safer without the computer. He knelt once again in prayer and slipped between the sheets, smiling. He felt better about himself than he had in a long time.

Kaitlyn, on her way to bed, opened the door and said good night.

"What's your favorite color?" he asked with a grin.

"Green," she answered, then continued on her way.

"It's going to be a good year," he said softly.

Got a Date with a Jewel Thief

In his first year working for the FBI in Chicago, 24-year-old Devin Mitchell was often assigned jobs nobody else wanted. Such was the case on that Friday afternoon in June when Blumenthal, his hard-nosed, square-jawed boss, called him into his office.

"I need you to transfer a suspect to Dallas today," Blumenthal said. "You'll be accompanying a female suspect we picked up yesterday. Her name is Maggie, alias 'Magic Fingers,' Steadman."

"Why is she called 'Magic Fingers?'"

"They say there's not a safe in the world she can't crack. We think she pulled off the jewel theft at the Bedford Museum in Dallas last year. She took more than half a million dollars in jewels, and did it without tripping the alarms."

"Sounds like she knew what she was doing."

Blumenthal had his back to him, looking out the window. "Steadman always knows what she's doing. But this time she made one mistake. She left a glove. We need to get her to Dallas to see if the glove fits. That's where you come in. Your plane leaves in two hours. Agent Baxter will pick her up at the county jail. He'll get her to Gate 89, Concourse 2, at three thirty, just before they start boarding the plane. We've made all the necessary arrangements with the airlines. Sorry to ruin any plans you might have made for the weekend, but that's the price we pay to work for the greatest law enforcement agency in the world."

"Yeah, right," Devin said.

Blumenthal whirled around to confront him. "Are you being cynical? Because I caught a little cynicism in your voice. You don't think we're the best law enforcement agency in the world? Is that what you're thinking?"

"No."

Blumenthal began to pace the floor. "Okay, I do admit that we've taken some hits lately in the media. And we may have made a few mistakes, but that doesn't detract from our past successes, does it?"

"No, sir, not at all."

"That's right. We just can't make any more mistakes, at least not any that the media can take advantage of. Listen to me, Mitchell, if you ever mess up, and there's a chance the media will get hold of it, I want to know about it right away. Do you understand?"

"I do."

"All right, get going."

Devin hurried to his apartment to pack. Stuck in traffic, he tried to call his mom on his cell phone to explain why he wouldn't be coming home for the weekend until Saturday. In the middle of his call, though, his cell phone died. He had been having trouble with it all week and had, just that morning, replaced the batteries. He decided to take it in to be fixed as soon as he got back from Dallas.

Just before leaving his apartment, he grabbed a couple of member missionary pass-along cards. Maybe I'll be able to give one of these away on my flight back tomorrow, he thought.

Meanwhile, Agent Baxter, with Maggie Steadman in his car, ran into traffic on the way to the airport. Traffic was slow enough, but adding to it was an accident between a semi-truck carrying aviation fuel and a pickup full of beehives. The beehives overturned on the highway, and that held up traffic for three hours.

At three-twenty-three, in front of Gate 89, Emily Gunnison, 23, also was waiting to board the flight to Dallas. She stopped to talk with a friend of her dad.

"Brother Stephenson, what are you doing here?"

"My son and his family are flying in for the weekend. What about you?"

"I'm going to Dallas to apply for a job."

"Good for you. What kind of a job?"

"I'm applying for a job with Homeland Security." She looked around. "A man who works for Homeland Security, who's going home for the weekend, is going to meet me here and fly down with me. He'll be briefing me about the job on our flight down."

"Well good luck, Emily! That reminds me of when I applied for my first job . . ."

Devin was late. By the time he arrived at the gate, most passengers had already boarded. He took a quick look around. An older gentleman and a young woman were the only twosome who had not boarded the plane.

They were announcing the final boarding for the flight when Devin walked up to the two still waiting. "I'll take over here," he said to the man. To the young woman, he said, "Let's go."

"I'm Emily Gunnison," she said. "And you are?"

He scoffed that she was using an alias. "Yeah, right, let's go."

On the plane, when they found their assigned seats, Devin insisted he have the aisle seat with Emily in the middle. "If you'll promise to keep your nose clean, we might be able to skip the handcuffs."

"My nose clean? Handcuffs? What are you talking about?"

Devin decided he needed to let her know who was boss. "What I'm talking about, sister, is you sitting down and keeping your yap shut." He gestured with his head for her to sit down.

She sat down. "That's what I was planning on doing."

"Okay, we'll see how it goes. But no monkey business, okay?"

"Monkey business?"

"Don't talk either," he said.

She glared at him. "Let me guess. You're having a bad day. Right?"

Half an hour into the flight, they announced they were about to show a movie. When the flight attendant came down the row with headphones, Devin shook his head. "No thanks."

"I'd like to see the movie," Emily said to the flight attendant, handing the cash to Devin for him to give it to her.

Devin kept the money and turned to the flight attendant. "She will not be watching the movie."

"What?" Emily asked.

"You heard what I said."

The flight attendant moved on.

"That's not fair," Emily complained.

"There's a lot in life that's not fair. For instance, breaking into a museum and taking half a million dollars in jewels. That's not fair to the people who put out hard-earned money for them. Did you ever think about that? By the way, Steadman, where did you hide the jewels from the Dallas job?"

Emily glared at him, then, surprisingly, started laughing. "Oh, I get it! This is some kind of a psychological test to see how I handle stress, right? Very good! Nicely done, too."

He looked at the cash she'd passed him to give to the flight attendant. "How much money do you have on you? Is it sewn into your clothes? How much? Ten thousand dollars? A hundred thousand dollars?"

"I don't think that's any of your business."

"Don't make me frisk you for it."

She reached over and touched her finger to his lips. "Let me give you a little advice. I understand you're doing this to get a personality profile on me. But I really think threatening to frisk me is a little over the top. Me being a woman, you being a guy, and we're not on government property. I really suspect that if CNN or the New York Times or the Chicago Tribune heard about this, they just might blow it all out of proportion. You know how the media is. Just a friendly bit of advice, that's all."

Devin panicked. She might have contacts, so he'd better be careful.

"Are we done with the psychological games now?" she asked.

"Yes, we are. Totally."

"Good." She started to read the in-flight magazine.

From the corner of his eye he sized her up, wondering how anyone would be able to guess she was an internationally famous jewel thief. He noticed that her fingers were long. He could imagine her opening a safe and grabbing the jewels in a museum while avoiding all the security devices.

He noticed a few other things about her that didn't have much to do with whether she was a jewel thief or not. She had long dark brown hair, thick black eyebrows, a long graceful neck, and dark olive-shaped eyes. He tried not to think about the fact that she was beautiful. That would be inappropriate. Even though she doesn't look it, she's a thief and a liar, he thought.

A few minutes later, she finished the magazine and returned it to its place. She turned to him and smiled. "Okay, now that you're done with the psychological testing, if you won't let me watch the movie, you're going to have to listen to me because I'm not just sitting here like a lump of coal until we get to Dallas."

"Yeah, sure," he grumbled. "Why don't you tell me about your tragic childhood. How you never had a chance in life. A sob story like that works with some people, but not with me though. But you go ahead and try if you want. You came from a rotten family, right?"

"Not really. My guess is you did though."

"This isn't about me, Lady."

"I came from a wonderful family. I have three brothers and two sisters. I'm the oldest. My dad was born and raised in Ashton, Idaho. My mom came from Waukegan, Illinois. They met when my dad was in the Navy. They met at a church dance and got married. After my dad got out of the Navy, they moved to Idaho. My dad took over the family farm. I came a year later."

Devin stared at her. Something's wrong. She looks like someone who could be a member of the Church. The way she dresses, the way she looks when she talks about her family. Is she that good of a con artist? And why do I think she's good looking? I'd better be careful here.

She continued. "I went to a small country school in Idaho. It was the perfect way to grow up." She sighed. "But when I was in seventh grade, my dad was killed in a farm accident. After a year, my mom decided to move back to Waukegan. And that's where I graduated from high school."

"What happened to turn you to a life of crime?"

She looked puzzled. "I . . ."

"You don't have to tell me all the sordid details. Just whatever you want."

"Well, after I graduated from high school, I went to college."

"Oh, sure, that's where it happened, isn't it? Let me guess. In college you met a guy, right? He was smart, and clever, and had lots of money. He asked you to help him out a little. At first it was easy, just going to a museum and finding out where the guards were, and when they changed shifts. Then he started to take you with him on his jobs. At first you didn't like it, but then after a while it got into your blood, and you liked the lifestyle, the excitement, the adrenaline rush. By that time, you couldn't quit."

"You have a rich fantasy life, don't you? Well, anyway, the truth is, I did meet a guy in college."

"And?"

"He went away."

"How long was he gone?"

"Two years."

"Well, that's not too bad. A lot of guys get sent away for a lot longer."

"Before he got back though, I went away."

"For how long?"

"Eighteen months."

"You must have had a good lawyer. So what happened to the guy?"

"He got married while I was gone."

"So because of him ditching you, you vowed to get revenge on the world, right?"

She shook her head. "You are the strangest person I've ever met."

"Hey, I may be strange but at least I'm not about to do time in a federal prison."

Her eyes brightened. "Really? Are you serious? Does that mean I got the job?"

He scoffed. "Oh yeah, you got the job, no problem there."

"That is such great news! I wonder what they'll have me doing there."

"It's a prison, okay? What do you think you'll be doing?"

"Oh, I don't know, filing, typing, routine clerical at first."

"Hey, I hate to burst your bubble, but the truth is, you're going to be making license plates."

She crinkled up her nose. "Isn't that what prisoners do?"

"Listen to me, Magic Fingers, you can put on that sweet innocent act for others, but don't try to con me, because I'm not buying it."

"Can I tell you something for your own good? You need counseling. I can't even begin to understand the depth of your problems, but I'm sure there's people who can help you work through this aggression you have for women. And, excuse me? Did you just call me Magic Fingers? What's that all about? Are we back to psychological games again?"

"Let's do each other a favor and not talk anymore."

"I think that would be a good idea." She sighed. "But first, there's one more thing I need to take care of. I know it doesn't make sense, but this morning in my prayers, I promised myself I'd do this." From her purse, she handed him a pass-along card.

In shock he stared at it. "Where'd you get this?"

"It's from my church."

His mouth dropped open. "From your church?"

"Yes."

"What's your name?"

"Emily Gunnison."

"So you're not Maggie Steadman?"

"No, why do you ask?"

"Could I see some identification?"

She handed him her driver's license. He studied it for a long time. As far as he could tell, it looked authentic.

He gave her a fake smile. "Could you excuse me for just a minute, please?"

"Yes, of course."

A minute later, after flashing his I.D., he was using an airlines-approved cell phone provided by one of the flight attendants.

"What happened to you?" Blumenthal asked. "We've been trying to get hold of you. Agent Baxter and 'Magic Fingers' got stuck in traffic so they missed the flight. We'll send Steadman with you on the next flight. Where are you now?"

Devin cleared his throat. "Well, actually, sir, I'm on the flight to Dallas."

"What, are you crazy? Why would you get on a flight without Steadman?"

"Well, actually, I thought Steadman was with me."

"How could she be with you if she was stuck in traffic?"

"I got to the airport late, and there was this man there, and he looked like he could be an agent, and there was this girl, and, well, she had long fingers so naturally I thought she was Steadman."

"You boarded the plane with a complete stranger?"

"She had a ticket to Dallas."

"You are an idiot! What have you done that could get us in trouble?"

"Nothing, nothing at all."

"So we're off the hook?" Blumenthal asked.

"Yeah, sure, no problem . . . except . . ."

"Except what?"

"She kind of wondered out loud if CNN might be interested in something I said to her."

"What did you say to her?"

"I sort of . . . uh . . . talked about . . . ah . . . that I might have to frisk her to see how much money she had."

"ARE YOU OUT OF YOUR MIND?"

"I didn't mean anything by it."

"You didn't mean anything by threatening to frisk a complete stranger, and a woman to boot? If this gets to the media, we'll never hear the end of it!"

"I think I can work things out with this girl."

"Why do you think that?"

"We both belong to the same church. I think I can win her over."

"You'd better win her over. If this gets to CNN, we'll both be fired. I don't care if it takes all weekend, I want you to make her your best friend. Maybe if you do that, she'll keep her mouth shut."

A short time later Devin returned to his seat. He gave her a big smile.

"Hey, anyone in the mood for a good movie?"

"No thanks. I've been lip reading the movie and it's not really that good."

He reached in his pocket and handed her a pass-along card. It was identical to the one she'd given him.

"You're handing back the card I gave you?"

"Oh, no, this is not your card. This is my card."

"You have a card?"

"I do. I just got back from a mission."

"You're kidding. I just got back from a mission. Are you married?" she asked.

"No way. How about you?"

"Same thing."

He gave her a cheesy smile. "You know what? I'd like to apologize for what I said to you before. You know, about saying I was going to frisk you. I hated to say that, but it's part of our in-flight psychological pre-assessment strategy."

"I figured as much. I hope I did okay. I've always wanted to work in law enforcement."

"You passed with flying colors. Good job!"

"That's great." She seemed to relax. "I was pretty sure it was some kind of a test, although there were a few times I thought you were certifiably crazy."

He smiled. "Yeah, I bet you did."

"What was the thing about the Magic Fingers?"

He forced himself to chuckle. "Oh, that! That was . . . a . . . test . . . designed to . . . make you think . . . that we didn't really have a clue who you were . . ." He laughed. "You know, like you were some kind of international jewel thief!" He forced himself to laugh again. "You know what? I was just talking to my boss. I told him how well you did. And do you know what he said?"

"No, what?"

"He told me that when we land, I should show you around Dallas tonight. No expenses spared. How does that sound to you?"

"Well, I don't care about spending a lot of money, but it would be fun to see the city." She paused. "I feel much better about you now."

"Sure, that's the ticket!"

After landing in Dallas, they took a taxi to her hotel. He booked a room on the same floor she was on.

They went to their rooms, changed clothes, and met in the lobby ten minutes later.

"You want to eat? I'm starving," he said. "I asked at the desk about fun places to eat, and I don't know if you'd be interested in this, but how would you like to go back to the Middle Ages and cheer for your favorite knight? As you dine, you'll see swordplay, falconry, horsemanship. The place is called Medieval Times. Whataya say?"

"Let's go!"

They had an amazing time together. They laughed, they talked, they ate wonderful food. Over dessert they talked about their families. On a horse-driven carriage ride around historic Dallas, they each told about their missions. At midnight, in the hotel cafe over a dish of ice cream, they talked about their hopes and dreams for the future.

On their way to her room, she patted his arm. "I suppose you were wondering why I never cheered for my favorite knight in the jousting tournament."

"Yeah, why was that?"

"I started to think that maybe, just maybe, my favorite knight was sitting right next to me."

When they reached her room, she opened the door. Standing on her tiptoes, she kissed him on the cheek, smiled, and said, "Good night, Devin. I had a great time."

"Me too."

He felt ecstatically happy until he got to his room, saw the flashing light on his phone, and a minute later found out from the hotel operator that Blumenthal had left him a message. "I don't care how late it is when you get in. Call me. I want to know what's going on with the girl."

He called the number Blumenthal had left.

"What?" Blumenthal answered on the first ring.

"Everything's good. I took her to dinner, and we talked. We have a lot in common. So, I think things went well. Tomorrow we're going to a couple of museums in town, so that'll be fun."

"Stick by her then and make her your friend."

"I'd like to stay with her until Tuesday morning, and then I'll fly back."

"Do what you have to. I just don't want to see any of this on CNN."

A few minutes later Devin, in his pajamas, sat on the edge of the bed holding the two pass-along cards in his hand. We have so much in common, he thought. I like it that her family is so important to her. And the way she crinkles her nose when she's confused—like when I called her Magic Fingers. And that she really does play the piano. And that she's served a mission. And that she's got a great laugh. That's the kind of girl I want someday, someone just like her.

On Saturday they spent the morning at the Dallas Museum of Art, where they also had lunch. In the afternoon they strolled through the Dallas Arboretum and Botanical Gardens.

Later that night they took in a baseball game, devouring hot dogs and chips for their dinner.

At eleven thirty they lingered at the door to her hotel room.

"I guess this is good night," she said.

"I guess so."

"I've never had a better time in my whole life," she said.

"Me either. It was really fun. I enjoyed being with you." He grinned. "This is kind of awkward, isn't it?"

"How's that?"

"You know, the both of us wondering if we're going to hug or kiss or just shake hands?"

"I can take care of that." She leaned forward to give him a hug, said goodnight, and went inside.

Sunday they took a taxi to a nearby ward. When they entered, a member of the bishopric stepped forward and shook their hands. "You folks just moved here?"

"Well, not really. We're just visiting."

"Good to have you here."

They sat down on one of the side benches. "He thought we were married," Devin said.

"I know. We should've told him we weren't."

"Yeah, although it does seem like a nice idea."

She laughed. "In case you've lost track, this is Day Three of Devin and Emily's Big Adventure."

"It seems like it's been longer."

"Is that a compliment or a complaint?"

"A compliment, I think."

After church they were invited to eat with a family in the ward, and stayed there until they were driven back to their hotel.

At the door, Devin gave her a good night kiss.

She sighed. "I suppose that was bound to happen. I just didn't think it would happen so soon."

"It's not that soon, actually. We've spent about thirty hours together this weekend. If we had spread that same amount of time over several dates, each one being about two hours, then we've had the equivalent of fifteen dates. And, also, if we went out once a week, then, essentially, we've known each other for about four months."

"Really, that long?"

"Run the numbers."

"Will you go with me in the morning to my interview?" she asked.

"If you want me to."

"Great. See you then."

The next morning during Emily's interview with Douglas B. Smythe, Devin waited in an outer office for her.

Twenty minutes later she came out of the office with a big smile on her face.

"Let me introduce you to the newest member of our team," Mr. Smythe said to Devin.

"Congratulations! That's great!"

"My interview today was very pleasant. A lot more pleasant than the pre-assessment psychological test on the plane," she said with a smile.

Smythe seemed confused.

"You know, where you're mistaken for Maggie Steadman, whoever she is, and you're treated like some kind of a criminal, and where Devin threatens to frisk you to see how much money you've got. You know, things like that."

"I have no idea what you're talking about," Smythe said. He then slowly turned his gaze from Emily to Devin. "What's going on here? Since when did we start doing psychological testing before we interview a candidate?"

That was all Emily needed. Her face was turning bright red and her jaw clenched. "Excuse me," she said, heading for the door.

"You still want the job?" Smythe called out.

"Yes, but I need to catch a flight home. I'll be to work in a week."

She left. Smythe glared at Devin. "Exactly what happened on the flight down here?"

Devin made a quick explanation to Smythe and then ran after Emily.

Just as he came running out of the building, he saw Emily in a taxi pulling away from the curb.

Devin flagged down another taxi. "Follow that car!"

He finally caught up with her at the hotel. She was nearly finished packing. Because a maid was doing cleanup in the room, the door was open.

"We need to talk!" Devin said, entering the room.

"I have nothing to say to you!"

"Let me explain."

"Okay, explain, and it better be good!"

"There really is a Maggie Steadman. She's a jewel thief. I was supposed to transport her to Dallas. There was a little bit of a mixup, and I thought you were Steadman. That's why I treated you so badly at first."

"And then what happened?"

"I called my boss and found out you weren't Steadman."

"And then?"

"Well, my boss was afraid you'd go to CNN and tell 'em how, once again, the FBI had messed up."

"So?"

"So he asked me to . . ." his voice trailed off.

"Be my friend? Win me over? Pretend you liked me? Talk about the possibility of us getting married?"

"No. All he asked me to do was to just try and be your friend."

Emily slammed the top of her suitcase shut. "So, in other words, you were paid for the time you spent with me! Is that right?"

Devin couldn't bear to answer the question, but he didn't need to. She could see the answer written on his face.

"Good bye, Devin," she said, grabbing her things and hurrying out the door.

"Wait! Let me explain!"

Waiting for the elevator, she put out her hand. "Don't come any closer and don't follow me any more or I'll have you arrested!"

"Something else happened."

"What?"

"I started to fall in love with you."

She shook her head. "You can't turn it off, can you? That's the worst lie you've told me since we met."

She left him standing in the hall.

Over the next few months, even after she moved to Dallas, he tried to contact her but she refused to speak with him. She returned his letters unopened, and never read any e-mails he sent her.

Every day he called and left a message apologizing, asking her to give him another chance. She never returned his calls.

Eventually he located her mom's address in Waukegan, Illinois. The day before Christmas, thinking that perhaps Emily would come home for the holidays, he drove to her mom's place. It was a modest brick house, built fifty years ago, identical to every other house on the block.

Devin knocked. A slender woman in her forties came to the door. "Yes?"

"My name is Devin Mitchell. I met Emily in the summer. Has she told you about me?"

Her mom frowned. "Yes, she's told me about you. What do you want?"

"I want to talk to Emily."

"She doesn't live here anymore."

"I thought she might have come home for the holidays."

"Like I said, she doesn't live here anymore."

"I keep trying to get in contact with her, but she won't talk to me. I was wondering if you could help me."

"I don't see how I can do anything to help you."

"Does she ever talk about me?"

"No, she never does. Not any more."

"I love her. I want to marry her."

"I'd say you'd have a better chance of marrying Maggie Steadman when she gets out of prison."

Devin glanced into the house and spotted a suitcase. It was the same one Emily had taken on her trip to Dallas.

She's here, he thought.

"Look, I'm not a bad person. I have a temple recommend. I do my home teaching. I earned my Eagle rank in scouting. I teach elders quorum in my ward, I can play the piano a little bit, but haven't practiced much lately. Look, if you want you can call my bishop to verify what I'm telling you."

The woman's expression softened. "Would you like to come in?" she said.

"Yes, thank you very much."

Although the TV was maybe thirty years old, and the sofa had seen better days, the best thing about the living room was an old upright piano.

"Please sit down and make yourself at home. I'll be just a minute."

Devin could hear Emily's mom talking with someone. A short time later Emily came into the living room. She put her hands on her hips in a classic 'Don't mess with me!' stance. "Show me your temple recommend."

He pulled it out and handed it to her. She looked it over to make sure it was current, nodded, and handed it back. "What was the lesson last week in priesthood and Relief Society?"

He told her.

"What was your favorite merit badge you earned in Scouting?"

"Lifesaving."

"See that piano? Go play me a song."

He stood up. "It's been a while."

"Play me a song."

"Why are we doing this?"

"I just want to know what percentage of the time you tell lies. So play the piano."

He played Clair de Lune for her.

"That wasn't too bad," she said. "So maybe you do play the piano. Go sit on the couch again."

He sat down. "You want the phone number of my bishop?"

"No." She sat down next to him and looked into his eyes. "You love me?"

"I do."

"You want to marry me?"

"I do."

She put her hand to her mouth and tapped her thumb to her teeth while she considered the idea. "You promise to keep your nose clean?"

"Yeah, sure."

"Okay, I think we can skip the handcuffs then," Emily said.

For the first time, Devin dared to smile. "Okay."

"You really think you're my knight in shining armor?"

"I want to be."

She pursed her lips. "And if we did get engaged, there would be no monkey business, right?"

"Absolutely none."

"Let me see your wallet."

He handed it over. She opened it, counted his money, and handed it back to him. "Would you have really frisked me?"

"No."

She nodded. "All right then, let's try it and see how it goes."

Now he was confused. "Try what?"

"Seeing each other again."

"Oh, okay."

They both sighed. "So . . ." he said. "Where do we start?"

"I don't know. I . . . uh . . . listened to the messages you left."

"And?"

"After a while I began to think you might not be such a bad guy, after all."

"Thanks."

The tension between them was gone, but by then Devin had a splitting headache. He mentioned it a few minutes later and she had him sit in a chair so she could massage his shoulders. His headache went away almost immediately. His first reaction was to tell her she really did have magic fingers, but he decided not to push his luck. He didn't want the ghost of Maggie Steadman hanging around their lives anymore. Even when his briefcase wouldn't open a few days later, and she picked the lock, he kept his mouth shut.

Three months later Devin and Emily were married.

Where You Go Depends on the Trail You Take

Zach should have known it was a mistake to let his older brother Michael, just home from BYU, to horn in on one of his neighborhood basketball games held in the driveway after school each day. In the first place, Michael, a returned missionary, was six years older than Zach and his friends, so he had a height and weight advantage.

The second mistake Zach made was letting Michael sit in when he and his friends had cookies and milk in the kitchen after their game. Michael didn't say much. Mainly he sat at the table and read a magazine. The other boys didn't pay much attention to him either, so eventually their conversation drifted to what it would have been if he hadn't been there.

"You going to Brittany's party Saturday night?" one of the boys asked Zach.

"Probably not."

"Why not? You should go. It's going to be a lot of fun. Her folks are going to be gone all weekend."

"So?"

"So she's getting a friend of hers to bring a keg of beer."

Zach looked at Michael to see if he was paying any attention to what was being said, but he seemed totally absorbed in his magazine.

"You guys know I don't drink," Zach said.

It was true he didn't drink, and he was pretty sure he'd never start, but lately it seemed all his friends from school were starting. It wasn't that Zach wanted to go against what he'd been taught all his life. It was just that he didn't want to be abandoned by his friends.

For some reason Michael, when he'd been in high school, although he'd kept the standards of the Church, hadn't seemed to have lost many of his friends. But Zach wasn't like his older brother. In fact, nobody was like Michael. He even wanted to teach seminary someday.

"Look, just try it once," a friend said. "If you don't like it, then at least you'll know."

"What if I do like it?" Zach asked.

"Then, no problem, you'll be more like us. It doesn't hurt anything to party once in a while."

Zach thought about it for a moment, then said, "I don't think it's for me, but thanks for asking."

"Look, Brittany asked me to invite you. She really likes you. I wouldn't be surprised if the only reason she's having a party is to get you to come and spend time with her."

Brittany was easily the best looking girl in school. If she was interested in him, Zach was definitely interested in her. "You really think so?"

"I'm sure of it. She cornered me today after class and made me promise to ask you to her party."

Zach smiled. This was the best news he'd had in a long time. "Maybe I'll go, at least for a while." And then he added for his own benefit. "But I won't drink."

"Yeah, right," one of his friends teased, "at least not until she asks you to have a drink. You know you won't turn her down. Whatever Brittany wants, she gets. And this weekend, she wants you."

Zach smiled. Brittany liked him!

After Zach's friends left, his brother didn't say anything about what he and his friends had talked about. Zach convinced himself that Michael hadn't been paying attention because if he'd heard, he'd have tried to talk Zach out of going to the party.

On Friday Michael asked him if he'd like to go hiking the next morning. Zach, who loved the outdoors, agreed to go.

Cloud Peak was ten miles from their home. The well-marked trail switched back and forth up the sides of the mountain. On the far side, a steep cliff dropped several hundred feet to the bottom.

They hiked about a third of the way to the top when they came to a place where the trail branched. One trail went downhill, the other continued to the top.

Michael stopped. "Let's take this other trail."

"What for?"

"It won't be as hard."

"That's because it goes downhill."

"Right. I'm tired of going up all the time. C'mon, just try it. You might like it." Without waiting for an answer, Michael headed down the other trail.

"What's going on? We'll never get to the top if we go downhill."

"C'mon, just try it. We'll worry about getting to the top later."

Zach thought his brother was crazy but followed him anyway. And he did have to admit it was easier hiking.

The trail wound around to the other side. Soon they were standing at the bottom of the sheer rock face which jutted to the top of the mountain. Strangely, there was a rope hanging down from the top.

"Okay, we've gone down far enough," Michael said. "Now let's climb to the top using the rope."

"You're crazy. It's too hard to climb straight up with a rope."

"It's possible to do it, though, right?" Michael asked.

"Yeah, sure, it's possible. It'd just be a lot harder."

"Got any suggestions how we can get to the top from here?"

"I don't see why you led us down here anyway. It would've been a lot easier just to stay on the trail."

"But it just kept going up. And the path we took to get here was very easy."

"But from here it will be too hard. I say we go back to where we left the trail heading up to the top."

"We can get to the top if we use the rope and pull ourselves up."

"I can't do it. My arms would give out."

"All right, look, let's just stay where we are then. I mean there's no rule that says we have to get to the top."

Zach threw his arms up in frustration. "We came here to climb to the top. So why did we end up here at the bottom? None of this makes any sense. This is the last time I'm ever going hiking with you. I mean it! You are so weird."

Michael thrust the rope at him. "Start climbing."

"I can't. It's too hard."

"Just a little ways," Michael said.

"Why is there a rope here anyway?"

"I put it here yesterday."

"What for?"

"Because there's a lesson to be learned from all this."

"Don't mess with me, Michael! Just tell me the stupid lesson and let's get out of here."

"Not until you climb at least part way up the rope."

"What are you, anyway? Mister Visual Aid?"

"There's a little piece of paper taped to a rock about ten feet up. Climb up there and get it."

"This is such a stupid waste of time!" Zach grabbed the rope and went hand over hand until he reached the all-important rock. He grabbed it and lowered himself down. Once he reached the ground, he looked at the paper. It read, Repentance.

"Repentance is always possible," Michael said, "but complete repentance is hard work. It takes a lot of effort to get back to where you were. It's better to stay on the trail that leads to the top."

Zach tore up the paper and threw it on the ground. "I hate this!" He started up the trail that would lead to the car. He had had it with his brother.

Michael followed after him. "Did you get the point of the lesson?"

"No, I didn't get anything!"

"If you want to get to the top, don't start going downhill just to see what it's like. For every step you go down, you'll have to go uphill on your way back. And you have no guarantee you'll have the self-discipline to make it back."

"Are you done?" Zach complained.

"Not quite."

Zach groaned. "What else?"

"Stay away from Brittany and her party tonight."

Zach blushed. "You were listening to us then, weren't you?"

"Yes. That's not the direction you want to go in your life, is it?"

Zach didn't answer for several minutes, then shrugged his shoulders. "No, it isn't the direction I want to go."

"Then stay on the path you're already on."

Zach nodded.

A few minutes later they reached the place where the trail divided. "Can we go home now?" Zach asked.

"No, we have to climb to the top to untie my rope."

At the top, after retrieving the rope, they sat together on a huge boulder and looked out at the valley below.

"It's nice at the top, isn't it?" Michael asked.

Zach turned and lightly slugged Michael on the shoulder. "All right! I won't go to the party tonight."

"You want to do something with me instead?" Michael asked.

"It won't have a lesson to it, will it?"

"No, not at all."

"What do you have in mind?" Zach asked.

"You ever been to Mystic Cave? It's about twenty miles from here. There's one part where it's totally dark. They have this iron railing you can hold onto. I thought we'd go there and turn off our flashlights. As long as we hold onto the iron rod, we'll be okay."

Zach started laughing. "You're totally out of control, you know that, don't you?"

"Just kidding. I'll save that for another time."

Instead they went roller blading in the Church parking lot. Afterwards they had pizza.

At the end of the night Zach had to admit he'd had a good time.

With no regrets.

Superman on Vacation

Memo to self: Beware of phone calls in the middle of the night.

"McKenzie, you're a sweet girl and everything, but I'm not going to be able to marry you next month like we planned."

"Curtis, I never said I'd marry you," I said. "At most, we're just good friends." Instead of just hanging up, which is what I usually did when he called, I asked, "Is anything wrong?"

"I just got arrested."

"Arrested? For what?"

"Armed robbery. I robbed a convenience store. I did it for you, so we'd have a nice honeymoon."

Not only did Curtis tell me this privately over the phone, he also told the media, making up a wild story about how we were engaged, and that I'd insisted on going to Hawaii for our honeymoon and told him I didn't care how he got the money.

My life became a living nightmare. Everywhere I went, someone was sticking a microphone in my face. Because of all the publicity, I left my apartment in Chicago and took a job as a summer intern at Yellowstone National Park, working in park security.

One week before the Fourth of July, I was on patrol when I saw a group of tourists calling out to a fisherman floating down the Yellowstone River. He apparently was unaware he was only a hundred yards from going over the Lower Falls, a three hundred foot drop which ends on very hard rocks.

I stopped my car, grabbed my bullhorn and pushed my way through the crowd to the edge of the river. "Sir, you're about to go over the falls. Come to the bank of the river immediately!"

The fisherman, a guy about my age, must not have understood me because he smiled and yelled, "Yeah, I got five so far!" He lifted up one of the fish for me to admire. "Look at this beauty!"

"Row to the bank of the river!"

Again, he either didn't hear me or didn't understand what I was saying. "I'm using a spinner!"

"Sir, listen to me! Get off the river!"

"What?"

"Come here!"

"What for?"

"You're about to go over the falls!"

"What falls?"

"The Lower Falls!"

"What? Just a minute. I think I've got a fish on my line."

"Sir, forget the stupid fish and get over here before it's too late!"

"Just a minute! This is a big fish!" He continued to reel in the fish on his line.

The crowd screamed as the boat went over the falls.

We spent until dark looking for the body. We found the boat crushed into a hundred pieces, but nothing else.

Just after nightfall I was exhausted as I made my way to my police car.

"What happened?" a guy standing by my car asked. He was approximately six foot two, weighed about 180 pounds, had brown eyes, a square jaw, and dark brown hair. He was wearing an oversized Yellowstone Park T-shirt, blue denim jeans, and hiking boots.

"A fisherman in a boat went over the falls."

"I'm sorry."

It had been long day and I felt awful. "I tried to warn him, but he didn't seem to understand me."

"Maybe he was just having a little fun at your expense."

"If that's true, then his so-called little fun cost him his life."

"Maybe not."

"Nobody could survive going over the falls."

"Suppose he had super-human powers, and he just wanted to have some fun. Someone with super human powers wouldn't get hurt by going over the falls. So maybe he thought it would be a good prank to pretend he didn't understand you when you were yelling for him to row to shore."

"Yeah, right, and maybe cows can fly. Look, sir, I'm very tired. Please excuse me."

"Wait, don't go. I'm the guy who was in the boat."

"No, you're not."

"You told me I was about to go over the falls and asked me to row to shore. I told you I'd caught five and showed you one of my fish. You told me to row to shore immediately, and I told you I was using a spinner."

"That doesn't prove you were the one in the boat. There was a crowd of people who watched this take place. All of them heard and saw what happened."

"Just after I went over the falls, you said softly, under your breath, 'Oh no, he's a goner. Why couldn't I make him understand?' That's why I came back. I felt sorry for you. You did a great job. I was just having a little fun with you, that's all."

"If you were in the boat, going over the falls, how could you possibly know what I said?"

He touched one of his ears. "Super hearing."

"Are you admitting you were the one who went over the falls?"

"Yes, of course. I came back to apologize."

"Sir, I am going to have put you under arrest."

"On what charge?"

I was so new that I had to make it up. "Going over the Lower Falls without a permit."

He suppressed a smile. "Without a permit? Where do you go to get a permit to go over those falls?"

This guy was making me mad. "I'd say it's a little late for getting a permit, sir."

"So, you're saying there's a law against going over the falls?"

"Yes, sir, there is. Section 102 of the Federal Code." Of course, I made it all up.

"How many people have ever been put behind bars for going over the falls without a permit?"

"I'm not sure I know the answer to that. But let me tell you, ten search and rescue personnel have spent the past several hours looking for your body. You've put people at risk looking for you. I'm only a summer intern, but I'm sure we can find a charge to hold you. Get in the vehicle. If you give me a hard time, I will be forced to put handcuffs on you."

"I am able to leap tall buildings with a single bound. So I could be in the next county before you knew what happened. I could also break any handcuffs you put on me."

"Yeah, whatever," I scoffed. "Get in the car, sir. We'll get you the psychological counseling you so desperately need."

"I will get in the car, but only because you interest me. Has anyone ever told you that you're good looking?"

I was in no mood for this. "Sir, I've had a rough day and I'm not in the mood to receive a compliment from someone who is clearly delusional."

On the way, I called my boss. "I have the guy who went over the falls."

"You need me to send somebody with a body bag?"

"He's not hurt. He's sitting here with me. He says he has superhuman powers."

A long pause. "Your sense of humor really gets whacked out when you're tired. Get some rest, McKenzie."

"I know it's impossible to go over the falls and not be killed. But if he did do it, is there a law on the books against going over the falls?"

"Not really. Anybody knows that if you did it, you'd die, so why have a law against it?"

The guy looked over at me and smirked.

"Well, there must be something I can arrest him for."

"Get some sleep. You're hallucinating."

"Wait a minute! I've got it! He had some fish in the boat. What's the limit just above the falls?"

"It's a catch-and-release area."

"That's what we'll get him for then! We'll throw the book at him."

"Okay, but we need the fish to make it stick."

I sighed. "The fish went over the falls with the boat. So I don't actually have them. I saw one of them though."

"No fish, no fine. Please get some sleep."

"I'm bringing him in for questioning."

"Well, you do what you want. I'm closing up shop. Even if you're not going to get any sleep tonight, I am."

"If you won't question him, then I will. And I will find something to charge him for."

"Be my guest. Turn off the lights when you leave."

Fifteen minutes later I led him to my boss's office and had him sit down. "Now let's get down to the bottom of this. Who are you?"

"My name is Clark Kent."

"Where are you from?"

"Well, I was born on another planet that has stronger gravity. That's why I'm so strong here."

I slowly brought my hand to my forehead. This guy was giving me such a headache. I needed to find something that would allow me to put him in a cell so I could go back to my apartment and get some sleep. "What about the boat? Where did you get the boat?"

"I bought it in Chicago yesterday."

"How did you get it here so fast?"

"I put it on my back and took a single bound. It's a lot like flying."

"So it was your boat?"

"Yes. I think I have a receipt for the boat in my wallet."

He gave me the receipt.

I had nothing to hold this guy except for the fact that he was crazy. And like my boss likes to say, "If we arrested every crazy tourist, there would be so many jails we'd have no room for the bears."

"All right, I give up," I said. "Get out of here. Do you need a ride back to your car?"

He gave me a superior look. "No, I'll be fine. Thanks. Good to meet you. Is there any chance we could hang out together while I'm here?"

"No, sir. I don't socialize with conceited selfish jerks who have problems distinguishing between reality and fantasy." I paused, thinking of Curtis, who fit that description completely.

"I've told you the truth about myself. In fact, you're the only one I've ever confided in, except for my step-parents. They found me when the space craft crashed near their farm."

"Whatever," I droned.

We were nearly out the door when the phone rang. I returned to my desk and answered it.

"Is this the park police?" an anxious voice asked.

"Yes, sir."

"There's been a terrible accident. I saw the whole thing. A car missed a curve and crashed into the side of the mountain. There's two people inside. They're both unconscious. We tried but we can't get them out of the car."

"Sir, where are you?"

Five minutes later I had all the information I needed. I called for an ambulance and a wrecker, and then headed for the door.

"Can I come with you? I might be able to help," Clark asked.

"No, we have it under control."

"I could get the two people out of the car."

I was surprised he knew what the caller had told me.

"Good day, sir," I said, brushing past him on my way to my car.

Twenty minutes later I pulled up to the crash scene, got out and surveyed the wreckage.

The tourist who'd called approached me. "I think one of them is still alive. I heard the woman in front groan, but I don't know about the driver. I haven't heard anything from him."

We went to the car. I tried to open the door but it wouldn't budge. "Sir, can you hear me? My name is Officer Pearson, I'm with the park police. Sir, we're going to get you and your companion out of here and to the hospital soon. Help is on the way."

Suddenly a tree a hundred feet away burst into flames. I and the man who'd called me both ran to my car. I grabbed a fire extinguisher and gave him a pick axe and we raced to put out the fire.

"What caused the fire?" the tourist asked.

"I'm not sure. Spark from the crash, I guess."

"That's some spark," the tourist said.

We put out the fire and then returned to the site of the crash. When we got there, the damaged car had been opened up like a tuna can, and the driver and passenger who'd been in the accident were gone.

"What's going on?" the tourist asked.

"I'm not sure. I need to call this in."

When I turned to head for my car, I noticed it wasn't there.

I used the tourist's cell phone and phoned my boss and told him what had happened. "MacKenzie, for the last time, would you get some sleep?"

I let him talk to the tourist who verified the story.

The tourist gave me his cell phone so I could wrap up my conversation with my boss.

My boss hadn't believed a word of it. "So, who's the guy on the phone? A friend of yours?"

I was tired of talking to him. I hung up.

I talked the tourist into giving me a ride back to my apartment.

As I thanked the man and headed for my place, Clark Kent was sitting on the top step of the place where summer interns stayed.

"I just thought you should know they're all right."

"What are you talking about?"

"The two in the accident. I was the one who started the tree on fire, and then I pried open the roof of the car, put the people in your car, and flew them to Salt Lake City. I figured they'd get good care there. And it's only a couple more seconds to get there."

"You're crazy!"

He smiled and handed me a cell phone, and gave me the number for the University of Utah Medical Center.

Ten minutes later I verified his story. The two in the accident were in the hospital in Salt Lake City and were recovering nicely.

"This can't be happening!" I complained.

"I know. It is hard to accept, isn't it?"

"What do you do with your powers?"

He shrugged. "Not much. Most of the time I don't use them at all."

"Why's that?"

"I think you know the answer to that."

"What are you talking about?"

"I didn't know it at first, but, I'm a newspaper reporter, and while I was waiting at the University of Utah Medical Center, I went through all the newspapers they have there. I saw your picture in the paper. I believe the headlines read, Bank Robber: I did it for my fiancé. That's you, isn't it?"

I sighed. Nobody in the park knew my history. "Yeah, that's me, but I'd appreciate it if you'd keep it quiet."

"Why would you want me to do that?"

"Because of all the reporters and TV news crews that will come here if anyone finds out where I am."

He smiled. "Relax, I won't tell anyone about you, if you won't tell anyone about me."

"It's a deal."

"I think now you can understand why I don't make my presence known. If I did, and the media found out who I was, I'd never have a moment's rest. They'd be camped outside my apartment 24/7."

"But if you don't use your powers to help others, then your life will have no meaning."

He shrugged his shoulders "You're right. My life has no meaning."

"What about getting married and having a family?"

He laughed at me. "Is this a proposal?"

"Not really. I'd never marry you."

"Why not?" he asked.

"I know your type. You're a man who thinks only about himself."

"I'm the strongest and fastest man in the world. I have X-ray vision, super-human hearing, and you're saying that's not enough? Anyone ever tell you that you're hard to please?"

"Lots of guys have told me that."

"Well, relax. I can't get married. If I do, then I automatically lose my super powers. It's one of the rules."

"Why's that?"

"If that didn't happen, then if I got married, my kids would be a super race that might take over the world. So I can't get married."

"So what do you do? Where do you work?" I asked.

"I'm a reporter for a newspaper. I report on crime but don't do anything to stop it. Because if I stopped it, then I'd become a national hero, and all my time would be taken up in front of the media."

"There's got to be some way you can help people without them knowing who you are."

"How?"

"I don't know." I yawned. "I've got to get some sleep. Can I give you a ride somewhere?"

"Not really. When I leave you, I'm going to fly to Alaska. I've got a place up there. It's made out of ice."

"Cheapskate," I teased.

"Can I see you tomorrow?" he asked.

"What for?"

"You're the only friend I've got."

"You work at a newspaper. You must have friends there."

"Not really."

"Okay, I guess we could get together after work."

He walked me to the door, said goodnight, then started walking down the road. Just after he was out of sight, I heard what sounded like a sonic boom and saw a glowing streak in the sky.

The next morning when I woke up, I suddenly knew how Clark Kent could help others without it ruining his life. I called in sick.

My boss was more than understanding. "You drove those two who were in the accident to Salt Lake City, didn't you? I just got a phone call from one of them, thanking us for saving their lives."

I tried not to lie. "Well, yes, they were in my car, and they did go to Salt Lake City. And, yes, it was a quick trip."

"You deserve a day off. You've earned it."

I called one of the secretaries who worked in the office and asked if I could borrow her sewing machine and some material. I told her I had the day off and had a sewing project I wanted to work on.

I worked all day.

At seven that night, Clark was at my door.

I invited him in and handed him the costume. "Put this on."

A few minutes later he came out of the bathroom. "You don't think it's a little too much?" he asked.

"No, I don't. It's perfect."

"What with the cape and the big S on my chest?" What's the S stand for?"

"Superman."

"You're kidding, right?"

"Not really. What else can we call you? Clark Kent Goes Theatrical? Trust me, it's got to be Superman."

"Okay, I'll try it."

A week later he brought me news about his first heroic deed. "So there was this little girl kidnaped and being kept in a garage not too far from Chicago, and because of my super hearing, I could hear her crying, so I knew where she was, and I busted into the place, and these two guys shot at me but the bullets bounced off my chest, and I grabbed them and tied them up, and called the police and waited for them to get there and arrest the two men and return the girl to her family. And it was great!"

"I'm so proud of you!"

From then on we didn't see much of each other. He kept busy saving people and stopping criminals. I returned to college in the fall. He visited me from time to time, always as Clark Kent.

Once when we were bored of sitting around eating bagels and drinking hot chocolate, he asked if I'd like to do something a little different. We started hiking. When we were away from people, he picked me up and we flew to San Francisco for dinner.

Over dessert, he reached over and held my hand. "I enjoy being with you. You're the only one I can be completely open with."

I sighed. "So, we really don't have a future then, do we?" I said.

"I guess not. I actually like being Superman—you know, helping people. You taught me the importance of service."

"You're doing a lot of good, that's for sure." I sighed.

"Anything wrong?"

"I was just thinking of the men who have been the heroes in my life. Like my dad. We were never rich. He worked two jobs to make sure we had food on the table and a roof over our heads. When I wanted to play soccer, he agreed to be our coach. He was always someone I could go to when I was having a hard time."

"Was?"

"He died three years ago. I really miss him. He was my hero. That's why I want to get married and be a mom and have a husband who will be a good dad. I wish you could experience that."

"I can't do both. This Superman gig keeps me unbelievably busy."

I nodded. "Of course it does, and you are doing a lot of good, too."

We took a leisurely flight back to my apartment. A short time later Clark and I were at the door.

"So, is this the end for us?" he asked.

"It might be."

"Can I kiss you?" he asked.

"I guess so."

He kissed me.

"That was some kiss," I whispered in his ear.

He laughed. "Well, I am Superman, you know."

"Don't let it go to your head," I teased. "It wasn't that great."

"Well, I held back."

"Yeah, me too," I joked.

He gave me a hug. We loved being in each other's arms.

"Who are you going to spend time with when you go back to work?" I asked.

"There is a new reporter. She's reasonably good looking."

"What's her name?"

"Lois Lane. She thinks I'm a nerd, though."

"That's good—for your disguise, I mean. I'm certainly not jealous, that's for sure."

"You're such a liar." He swept back a few strands of hair that had gotten out of place. "This is hard, isn't it?"

"It is. It's very hard. You're my best friend, you're my hero, and I'm in love with you."

"And that's not enough?" he asked.

"No, it's not. I want to be married and have a family."

He kissed me on the cheek. "Take care, okay? I'll come and visit you real soon."

Six months later, he still had not come to see me. I kept up with his many deeds on TV and in newspapers. Hardly a day went by when he wasn't in the news, breaking up bank robberies, saving kidnaped children, using his super breath to put out a raging forest fire.

But then suddenly without warning, in early May, Superman dropped out of sight. The media spent countless days speculating on what might have happened.

I went to the library and looked at all the past issues of the newspaper where Clark worked. About the same time Superman disappeared, Clark Kent quit writing for the newspaper. I called the editor and he told me Clark had quit.

Fox News reported that Superman had taken a job working for the CIA trying to fight terrorism, and had been killed. CNN reported Superman had been an alien, like E.T, and had returned back to his planet. Rumors were all over the place.

A week later I went back to Yellowstone Park to work again, this time not in security but as a park ranger. My job was to give nature lectures at night at Old Faithful.

I liked to start each lecture by finding out where people were from.

"Oklahoma!" a man shouted.

"Great, who else?" I asked, glancing down at the console as I prepared to dim the lights and start the slide show.

"Chicago!"

The voice was unmistakable. I looked up and there he was—Clark Kent.

"Tell us a little about you, Clark."

"I'm just an ordinary guy, with ordinary powers, who's hoping to find a girl and settle down and get married."

In front of all the tourists, I ran to him and threw my arms around him and kissed him.

"Whoa!" he said when we broke away. "This is sure a friendly park!"

"You have no idea!" I said, as we both started to laugh.

Four weeks later we were married.

Clark is no Superman these days, but, you know what?—he will always be my hero, and I know he will be a hero to our children, of which one is now on the way.

And, that, after all, is what life is all about.

Just Friends

Dave and Rachel were, with thirty others in their campus ward at BYU-Idaho, waiting for the room to clear out so they could go to their Sunday School class. Dave was only a couple of inches taller than Rachel. They had both played basketball in their high schools and had both hurt their knees so neither one of them played much anymore.

"I'm in charge of a game for home evening for tomorrow night," Rachel said. "What would you like to play?"

Dave shrugged. "It doesn't really matter to me."

"What would you think about playing 'In the Manner of the Adverb'?"

He yawned. "We always play that."

"We haven't played it this semester."

"It seems like we play it every other week."

"Nope, we haven't. I've kept track of what we do every week."

Rachel had long red hair, a fair complexion, and blue eyes. Dave once told her she reminded him of a girl in the last branch he'd served in on his mission to Scotland. "She was a bonnie girl, too, that one, except she was only thirteen," he said with his best Scottish accent.

Rachel's back was leaning against the wall. Dave put his hand out to lean on the wall. It allowed him to be closer to Rachel than he otherwise would have done. "Sometimes I feel like I've been in this ward all my life."

"Just two years."

"It seems way longer than that to me."

She nodded. "I know what you mean." She sighed. "Actually, this will probably be my last semester here."

"Really? How come?"

"I've been thinking about going on a mission. I turn twenty-one in August, so if I'm going to go, I might as well go then."

"You've never talked about going on a mission before."

"Well, it's not like we're that close," she said.

"We're together all the time, for home evening, ward prayer, church on Sundays, and ward activities."

"What I mean is," she said, "I haven't noticed either one of us sharing our hopes and dreams with each other."

"That's because I don't have any. I just take each day as it comes. I never plan ahead."

"I'm not sure I believe that."

"Ask anyone," he said. "They'll all tell you how shallow I am." He winked at her and smiled.

People started to file into the classroom. "It's time for class."

"You're seriously thinking about serving a mission?" he asked as they followed the other students inside.

"You served a mission, right? So what's wrong for me to want the same blessings you enjoyed?"

"Nothing, nothing at all. Go for it, if that's what you want."

"I got the papers from the bishop this morning. I'm getting my dental and medical exams in the next few days, so with any luck, I'll be submitting my papers in a week. In fact, I hope to meet with President Miller next Sunday."

They made their way into the room. For the first time in a long time, Dave did not sit next to Rachel.

After church, in his apartment, Dave paced the floor while Alex, his roommate, talked on the phone with his family.

After Alex hung up, Dave said, "Rachel is thinking about going on a mission. Can you believe that?"

"So, what do you care if she goes on a mission or not?"

"I don't care."

"Great."

"It's just that I didn't know she was even thinking about serving a mission, that's all."

"So what's the big deal?" Alex turned and looked into Dave's eyes. "Do you like her?"

"Sure. Everybody likes Rachel."

"So you don't like her more than any other girl in the ward?"

"No, not really . . . well, maybe a little more than most girls. I don't know. I haven't thought about it much. She's always there for me, you know what I mean?"

"I do. Does she know you like her?"

"Sure, she does. I mean, we've been in the same home evening group for the past two years."

"Have you ever told her you like her?"

"No, not in so many words, but she knows."

"Really? I'm your roommate, and I didn't know you liked her, so how could she possibly know?"

"Look, for your information, I've gone to every home evening for the last two years. That should tell her something, right?"

Alex threw his hands in the air. "Whoa! Well, that's it then! One hundred percent home evening attendance! If that isn't true love, what is?"

"Love?" Dave asked. "How did love get into this discussion? All I'm saying is I didn't know she was thinking about going on a mission."

Alex shook his head and started a letter while Dave stood behind him with his mouth open and his gaze fixed on the floor.

After a few minutes Alex turned around. "Look, isn't there some place you need to be? You're really spooking me just standing there."

At the same time, Rachel was talking with her roommate Vanessa. "Today I told Dave I was planning on going on a mission."

"What did he say?"

"He said he didn't know I was thinking about that."

"That's all he said?"

Rachel nodded. "He doesn't care if I go or not."

"He likes you."

"How can you say that? He's never asked me out."

"He always manages to sit next to you at home evening."

Rachel shrugged. "He has to sit somewhere."

"There was that one time he rested his head on your shoulder."

"You mean when he fell asleep during the lesson? That doesn't count. In fact, I'm not sitting next to him anymore."

"Why would you do that?"

"He didn't sit next to me in Sunday School."

At home evening the next night, Rachel made sure she didn't sit next to Dave. Jordan, a freshman girl with the reputation of being willing to bake cookies for any guy in the ward, did sit next to him.

After home evening, as everyone was leaving, Jordan said to Dave, "I'll bring you some cookies in a few minutes!"

"What a tramp," Rachel complained to Vanessa under her breath.

In their apartment after home evening, Rachel cornered Vanessa. "Jordan can bake him cookies every day for the rest of the semester for all I care. But I'm not baking him cookies, do you hear? Not a single cookie! Besides, what do I care? I'm going on a mission."

About an hour later, Dave, in his apartment, was complaining to Alex. "Rachel didn't even sit with me at home evening."

Alex was munching on the cookies Jordan had just brought over. "I'd say it all turned out for the best. We got cookies out of the deal, didn't we?"

"Why didn't Rachel want to sit with me?" Dave asked.

"Maybe she's afraid you really like her, and that you'll try to talk her out of serving a mission."

"Look, let's get one thing straight! I don't care if she serves a mission or not. It makes absolutely no difference to me one way or the other." He stood up. "I'm going to take a walk now."

"Good, take one for me. I think I'll polish off the rest of these cookies and then read scriptures."

An hour later Dave returned from his walk. Alex was sleeping at his desk, his forehead resting on his open Bible.

Dave pulled his chair up next to him. "You asleep?"

"Uh," Alex muttered.

"I've decided something. I'm definitely not in love with Rachel. I like her, of course, but that's all. We're just good friends."

"Ah," Alex replied in his sleep.

"It is true that she's the best-looking girl I've ever known. Maybe not everyone sees it that way, but I do. I don't know if you've ever noticed it, but she crinkles her nose when she smiles. And her skin is, well, I don't know how to describe it, but it's very white. It's like she's been locked up in a prison all her life. And her hair, well, I don't need to tell you about her hair. It's red, you know. But it's not coarse like mine. It's more like corn silk. She's a good person too. Did you know she pays tithing on her scholarship? I've never heard of that. I tried to talk her out of it but she wouldn't budge."

"Ah," Alex said, still asleep.

"Sometimes when I'm not thinking clearly . . . well, I can almost talk myself into thinking . . . that I . . . that I could be . . . I mean, it's possible . . . that I might possibly be in love with her. Dumb, huh? The mind plays strange tricks sometimes, doesn't it?"

"Ah," Alex said.

"I'm glad we've been able to talk about this. Just don't tell anyone, okay?"

"Uh-huh."

At the same time in Rachel's apartment, something equally significant was occurring. Vanessa went into the kitchen and found Rachel cracking an egg into a mixing bowl. "What are you doing?"

"I'm making cookies," Rachel snapped. "I'm warning you! Don't say another word!"

"You're making cookies for Dave?"

"I don't want to talk about it!"

"Why would you make cookies for Dave?"

"I can make cookies for anyone I please! I'm just a little out of practice, that's all. I haven't done it since I was a freshman."

"Actually, you're supposed to put the chocolate chips in with the cookie dough, not eat 'em out of the bag. Just a little hint."

"You think I don't know that?"

Trying to sound like a police officer, Vanessa called out, "Ma'am, I'm afraid I'm going to have to ask you to step away from the bag of chocolate chips and put down your spoon and come with me." And then Vanessa grabbed Rachel's wrist and started to pull her out of the kitchen. "Come with me, Ma'am."

"What are you doing?"

"We really need to talk."

They ended up in their room, sitting on their beds across from each other.

"You can't turn in your papers until you and Dave have had a talk."

"A talk about what?"

"About your relationship."

"We don't have a relationship. We're just friends."

"I think you do have a relationship," Vanessa said. "You just haven't admitted it to each other."

They talked for another hour. By the time they finished, Rachel agreed to meet with President Miller and let him know she wasn't ready to turn in her papers yet.

Vanessa then helped Rachel bake the cookies. They delivered them to Dave later that night even though it was nearly curfew.

When he opened the door, Rachel thrust the cookies into his hand. "I baked these for you. Bye."

After having one cookie, Dave called his mother to talk to her about Rachel.

Her advice was, "If you have feelings for the girl, you've got to tell her."

"But what right do I have to try to talk her out of serving a mission?"

"Don't talk her out of anything. Just tell her how you feel."

"I'm not sure how I feel."

"Do you love her?"

A long pause. "It's possible, I guess, but I'm not sure."

"Then tell her that."

"She'll think I'm an idiot."

"If you don't tell her, she'll never know how you feel. If you do, she's free to make whatever decision she wants."

On Tuesday night, Dave called and asked to speak with Rachel.

"She's meeting with the stake president," another roommate said.

"What? How can she have filled out her papers so soon?"

"I don't know. I was gone all weekend."

Dave burst into the room where Alex was studying. "Rachel's meeting right now with President Miller to turn in her papers!"

"How'd she get her dental and medical done so fast? It took me three weeks, and my mom helped me."

"It's too late now, isn't it? Once she turns in her papers, it's too late."

"It's never too late," Alex said. "But you got to go talk to her now, before it's too late."

"I thought you said it was never too late."

"Don't argue with me. Go! Hurry up!"

Five minutes later, gasping for breath because he'd run across campus, Dave knocked on President Miller's door.

The president himself answered. "Yes?"

Dave looked in and saw Rachel. "Rachel, we've got to talk! Right away, before you turn in your papers."

"But . . . I . . ."

"Don't argue. Just come out in the hall and talk with me. Then, if you have to, then you can go back and turn in your papers."

Rachel looked at President Miller, who smiled and nodded.

Dave escorted her down the hall until he found a place where they could be alone.

"What's on your mind?" she asked.

"Let me put it this way. Your right knee is shot, and, for me, it's my left knee. So, if you think about it, between the two of us, we've got one good set . . . of knees."

Slowly her mouth dropped open. "Am I supposed to understand what you just said?"

"Look, what I'm trying to say is don't turn in your papers yet. I think we should see each other first."

"We see each other all the time."

Dave cleared his throat. "What I mean is, we should go to a movie or a dance."

"You mean both of our apartments? Like a group date? Like we've done a hundred times before?"

"No, not like that! Just you and me."

She nervously ran her fingers through her hair. "Just the two of us?"

"That's right."

"What for?" she asked.

"Let me think about that for a minute, okay?"

"Take all the time you need."

He took a long drink at the water fountain. "To see how we like being alone . . . together."

"And that would be important because . . . ?" she asked.

"Well, there's a possibility that, well, that you and me . . . I mean, that you and I, might—this is so hard!"

"You want to think about it overnight and then get back to me?" she asked.

"No, just let me say it."

"Okay."

He shook his head. "This is so stupid. You're going to think I'm an idiot."

"I don't think this is going to change my opinion of you, Dave."

He fought back a grin. "Does that mean you've always thought I was an idiot?"

"No, what it means is, we're friends and we'll always be friends. So just tell me what's on your mind."

"There's a distinct possibility that I have feelings for you."

"What kind of feelings?"

He shook his head. "Well, as near as I can tell, feelings of, well, love I guess."

"Love?"

"It's possible. And if that is the case, then I'd prefer it if you didn't serve a mission. Okay, I know my timing stinks because you're here tonight to turn in your papers, but I called my mom and she said that I needed to tell you how I feel about you. At first I didn't even know how I felt for sure, but I've thought about it a lot, and I think it's very likely that I may be in love with you . . . or could be if we spent some time together, just the two of us."

"So you came here tonight to try and talk me out of turning in my papers. Is that right?"

He nodded. "It sounds really selfish of me, doesn't it? But, to be honest, that's the way I feel."

"I see."

"The way I figure it we'd have to see each other on nights other than home evening and Sundays and ward activities," he said.

"I see. Alone, just the two of us then?"

"That's right."

She pursed her lips. "Well, okay. Let's try it and see how it works out."

They started back to the stake president's office. "I have a little confession to make," she said. "I wasn't here to turn in my papers. I came to say that I needed more time to decide if I even want to serve a mission, because I wanted to find out about us."

"So I didn't need to come here after all?"

"No, but I'm glad you did. The way you burst through the door was very dramatic."

"I knocked first."

"The important thing is you came, not knowing how this would turn out. It's very flattering that you'd do that for me."

"In a way I guess you could say we're in new territory," he said.

She nodded. "They have a name for it."

"What's the name? Fumbling around? Trying to find our way?"

"No, they call it courtship."

"I've heard of it, but I've never done it."

She smiled. "I guess we'll learn about it together then, won't we? Don't worry, we'll have each other to lean on . . . and we have two good knees between us."

"If this works out, it could lead to . . ."

"What?"

"I'm not sure if I should say it."

"Go ahead, say it."

"It could lead to marriage." He wiped the perspiration from his forehead.

"You're right. It could lead to that."

"I need another drink," he said, using the water fountain again.

"You okay?" she asked.

"Yeah, I'm okay. Don't worry about me."

"Is there anything I can do for you?"

He shook his head, then changed his mind. "Could you bring me some more cookies sometime soon?"

"Sure, big guy, whatever you want."

They approached the stake president's office holding hands.

Just Seeing Each Other

[*This story is the continuation of "Just Friends."*]

After three weeks of just seeing each other, Dave and Rachel had moved beyond the 'just good friends' stage.

"Last night during the movie, you kissed me," Rachel said to Dave as they walked to church.

"Yeah, so?"

"What was that all about? In terms of our relationship, I mean."

"I wasn't really thinking about it in terms of our relationship."

"How were you thinking of it then?" she asked.

"I don't know. It was just something I wanted to do."

"That's the only reason you kissed me?" she asked. "Just because you wanted to?"

Dave cleared his throat, realizing he was in hostile territory. "No, of course not."

"What were the other reasons?"

Dave was clueless about what she wanted him to say. "Well, you know, our relationship . . . and everything."

"What about our relationship?"

"It's good . . . real good," he stammered.

"Good in what way?"

"Well, we're more than just friends now."

"So that justifies us kissing? See, I don't look at it that way."

He groaned. "Why isn't that a surprise to me? Tell me, how do you look at it?"

"Well, it's true we are better friends than we were but, the way I see it, we're still not close enough to be kissing, and especially not in a movie theater, with who knows how many people watching us."

"We were in the back of the theater and it was during a fight scene. So who was watching us?"

"It just came out of nowhere. I mean, I'm sitting there, watching the movie, and then all of a sudden, pow, I'm being kissed. I still had butter on my face from the popcorn."

"Yeah, me too. They should give away baby-wipes with each box of popcorn."

"You've never even told me how you feel about me," she said.

"I must like you, right? I'm still asking you out."

"I'm sorry, but that isn't good enough for me."

"What do you want from me?" he asked.

"I want to know where this is going."

"How should I know where it's going?" he grumbled. "I like you more than I used to. A lot more in fact."

She shook her head. "Look, don't ever try to kiss me in a movie theater again, okay?"

"Yeah, sure."

"All right then."

After a long pause, Dave asked, "Where do you want me to kiss you, then?"

"Do we have to talk about this just before church?"

Dave had had it. "No, we don't have to ever talk about this again. In fact, we don't even need to keep seeing each other, if that's what you want."

"No, that's not what I want."

"What do you want then, Rachel? I can't ever understand what you want."

"I want to know where this is going."

"In terms of our relationship, you mean?"

"Yes," she said.

"Well, I'm not sure, except there's nobody else I'd rather be with than you."

She smiled and leaned into him. "I feel the same way."

"Okay then, let's keep seeing each other."

"The next time you're thinking of kissing me, at least say something nice to me," she said.

"Like what?"

She thought about it. "How about saying that I'm important to you?"

He smiled. "Oh, I get it. It's like some kind of secret code then, right?"

Rachel sighed. "I guess so, if that's the way you want to look at it."

Three weeks later they were in her apartment watching a movie with her roommate Vanessa.

Vanessa left to use the bathroom.

"You're very important to me," Dave said.

"Yeah, whatever," Rachel said, practically leaping into his arms.

When Vanessa returned, they separated. Vanessa went next door to borrow some microwave popcorn.

"This isn't good, us being alone like this," Rachel said.

"That's why we started seeing each other, so we could be alone."

"We can't be alone now though," she said. "We're in a new stage in our relationship."

"What stage is that?"

"The stage where we can't be alone."

Vanessa returned, made popcorn, which the three of them ate. Then Vanessa said, "I need to go to the library and check out some books."

"No! Don't go!" Rachel pleaded.

"That's right!" Dave added. "If you have any compassion in your heart, don't go. Stay here and talk with us. What classes are you taking?"

"And how are you doing in them?" Rachel added.

"Why are you two so interested in my classes?"

"It's not just your classes we're interested in," Dave said. "We want to know everything about you. Where were you born?"

"Cleveland."

"Cleveland?" Dave shouted. "Did you say Cleveland? I can't believe it! Rachel, Vanessa here was born in Cleveland! Isn't that amazing?"

Vanessa's mouth dropped open. "Why are you so interested in Cleveland? Were either of you born there?"

"No, not really, but I've heard it's a nice town."

Vanessa stood up. "I'm going to the library now."

"You can't go now!" Rachel called out.

"Why not?"

They both blushed. "If you go, we'll be in the apartment all alone," Dave finally admitted.

"I don't get it," Vanessa said. "You guys like to be alone together."

"Well . . . yes . . . initially that was true . . . but now things are . . . well . . . different," Rachel said.

Finally it dawned on Vanessa. "You guys need a chaperone?"

Dave blushed and lowered his gaze.

"That's right," Rachel said. "We need a chaperone."

"Oh, sorry, I didn't know. I'll stay then."

Over the next two weeks, they learned a great deal about Vanessa.

One week after that, Dave, in passing, mentioned the M word to Rachel. "If things continue as they've been going, then, maybe, at some time, we might want to think about talking about, well, getting married."

"Was that a proposal? Because if it was, it was really lame."

"It wasn't a proposal. It was just a thought."

"So, do you want to talk about getting married?" she asked.

"In general terms, I guess so."

"If we're talking about getting married, then you'd better meet my folks."

"Is that absolutely necessary?" he asked.

"Yes, I want them to know who you are. Why don't you come home with me over spring break?"

And so Wednesday, April 2, saw them on the road.

"Should I be worried about meeting your folks?" Dave asked as they entered Salem, Oregon.

"No, not at all. In fact, they're looking forward to meeting you. You have nothing to worry about."

"I hope you're right. I'm really nervous."

"Don't be. I've told them all about you so they already like you. Take a left at the next light."

"Tell me about your dad."

She hesitated. "Well, he keeps busy," she said vaguely.

"What does he do?"

"Oh, you know, legal things, mostly."

"So, he's a lawyer."

"Sort of." She sighed. "Well, actually, he's on the Oregon Supreme Court."

Dave laughed. "Seriously, what does he do?"

"That's what he does."

Dave instinctively put his foot on the brake. "Why didn't you tell me this before now?" he complained.

"Relax. At home, he's just my dad. Don't worry about it."

"Tell me about your mom."

"Well, she likes to cook and sew and she loves her flower garden."

Dave nodded. "That sounds like my mom."

"She works part time in real estate."

"So, she sells houses in her spare time?" he asked.

"Something like that. Turn left at the stop sign."

"What exactly is your mom's job?"

"Well, she has own her own real estate company. So that's good, right? That way she doesn't have to work all the time."

Dave shook his head. "Your mom and dad are going to hate me."

Half an hour later they pulled into a gated community in an exclusive suburb of Salem. To get through the gate Rachel had to swipe a card through a reader.

They drove for a minute before Dave noticed a large three-story building on the top of a hill. "What's that, a hotel?"

"No, that's home."

"That's your home?"

Dave drove slowly toward the house on the hill.

"Don't get quiet on me," she said. "I hate it when you won't tell me what you're thinking. It's going to be okay. You'll see."

And it was okay, at least for the first few minutes, with questions like, How was your trip? How were the roads? Where are you from? Have you ever been to Oregon before? How many brothers and sisters do you have?

They had a pleasant supper, but just before dessert, Rachel's dad got down to business. "What year in school are you?"

"I'm a sophomore."

"I see. And what are you majoring in?"

"At first I was majoring in music, but during my mission I decided that wasn't very practical, so after I got back from my mission I switched to art history."

There was a painful silence in the room.

"Art history? Really? How wonderful!" Rachel's mom said cheerfully. "We've always loved art, haven't we, Edward?"

"You switched from music to art history because it was more practical. Tell me, is there a lot of demand for people who can do art history?"

Dave grabbed the pitcher of water and poured himself another glass of water. "No, that's just it, there's no demand. So a couple of weeks ago I switched to landscape architecture." He quickly drained his glass of water.

"Well, that's very practical," Rachel's mom said brightly. "What made you think of majoring in that?"

"In high school I mowed lawns in the summers, and I really liked that."

"Mowing lawns?" Rachel's dad asked. "Is that what you'd like to do for your full time job?"

"Well, sure, if it paid enough money."

"We pay the boy who mows our lawn fifty dollars a week," Rachel's mom said.

"You have a big lawn though," Dave said. "Usually I'd get somewhere between fifteen and twenty five dollars a week."

"It's a free country," Rachel's dad said gruffly. "If you want to mow lawns for the rest of your life, then do it."

"Well, of course I know I couldn't make enough to feed a family mowing lawns."

"So what are you going to do? Throw in some edging, maybe a little weed whacking?"

"Daddy, don't be so mean," Rachel said.

"Look, David, you do whatever you want," her father said, "and be sure to write us from time to time. Let us know how you're doing."

Rachel reached for Dave's hand. "Well, it's very possible you and Mom will always know what Dave is doing, so he won't have to write."

"Why should we know what he's doing?" her dad asked. "Is he moving to Salem?"

"Dave and I are talking about getting married," Rachel said.

"To each other?" her dad asked. His eyes widened. "Did you know about this?" he quizzed his wife.

"I knew they were seeing each other. Rachel asked for my recipe for chocolate chip cookies."

"We wanted to surprise you," Rachel said.

"Oh, well, you certainly have surprised us! Yes, I would say that you have certainly surprised us." Edward turned his cold grey eyes on Dave. "I wonder if we might talk privately in my study before we have dessert."

"If you'd like."

In the huge study, with a large mahogany desk and a book case that covered one entire wall, Edward asked Dave to sit down. "May I, in all frankness, ask you a few questions?"

"I guess so," Dave said, wiping the perspiration from his forehead.

"Have you served a mission?"

"Yes."

"Do you have a current temple recommend?"

"Yes."

Edward seemed to relax a little. "You seem like a worthwhile young man. I might, in due time, be persuaded to give you permission to marry my daughter. There's just one thing though. We've always valued education. We'd like Rachel to finish college before she gets married. That's about a year and a half away. I'm sure you'd be willing to wait just that little time."

Dave swallowed hard. "A year and a half?"

"Yes, that's right. The time will go quickly."

"Actually, sir, with all due respect, I'm not sure we'd be able to wait that long."

"I don't understand. Why wouldn't you be able to wait?"

"Well, hormones, I guess you could say."

"Hormones? Is that what you said? You're basing a decision about when to get married on hormones?"

"Well, the way I look at it, we could get married in a year and a half, but chances are it wouldn't be in the temple. What I'm trying to say is that there are certain pressures."

Edward got up from his desk and began to pace back and forth. "Let me see if I understand what I've learned from you so far. Given a choice of a career, your first choice would be to mow lawns. And the reason why you can't wait until she finishes college is because of your raging hormones? Am I representing your position accurately?"

"I don't think a long engagement is going to work for us, sir. I mean, even now we have to be very careful all the time. We only kiss at the door with Rachel's hand on the doorknob so she can make a quick get-away. I mean it's really getting difficult."

"My wife and I were engaged a year before we got married and we had absolutely no problems at all."

"Well, that's great, but I don't think it's going to work for us. I'm twenty-two years old. Rachel is nearly twenty-one. We're in love, so for us, it's time to get married."

"What if, right after you get married, she gets pregnant."

"Then I suppose we'll have a baby nine months later."

"And how are you going to support a wife and a baby? Collect aluminum cans?"

Dave stood up. "Well, sir, it's been great talking to you. I'm going back for dessert now."

"We're not through here."

"You may not be through, sir, but I am." With that, Dave returned to the dining room.

They had an awkward but very polite dessert. After her offer to help clean up was refused, Rachel and Dave went outside and shot baskets while her folks worked in the kitchen.

Unfortunately the exhaust fan for the kitchen vented not far from the basketball hoop, and since the fan was not on, they could hear everything her folks said.

"I can't believe it!" Edward raged. "He's going to mow lawns for a living? What kind of a life is that going to be for Rachel? He's got no drive to make something of his life, and he admitted it himself—raging hormones. Five thousand guys at BYU-Idaho and she picks him? Unbelievable! In my day we had professional goals. We had self-control. You and I were engaged a full year and we never had any problems."

"It was only six months."

"No, I'm sure it was longer than that."

"It was six months. You were in law school in New York. I was in Utah. It wasn't so much self-control as it was geography."

Rachel started laughing. "Let's get away from here and take a walk."

They held hands as they walked. It made everything better.

"Meeting your folks so far has been a disaster. Your dad hates me."

"That's ridiculous. He doesn't know you well enough to hate you."

"He makes me feel like a real loser."

"Well, you're not." She leaned over and kissed him on the cheek. "There's nobody in the whole world I'd rather be with than you."

"That's the way I feel about you. You're the best friend I've ever had."

"Thank you."

After a pause, he asked, "Am I the best friend you've ever had?"

"The best guy friend I've ever had. And not only that, but I love you."

"I love you, too."

Suddenly he escorted her off the path. "Come with me."

"What's going on?"

"A surprise."

In a secluded wooded area, he knelt down and took her hand. "Rachel, will you marry me?"

"What?"

"I'm proposing to you." He reached in his front pocket and pulled out a ring, slipping it on her finger. "Will you marry me?"

"Is this official?"

"It is. I love you with all my heart. I want to spend the rest of eternity with you."

She started to cry.

"That isn't a good sign, is it?" he asked.

"No, it is. These are tears of happiness. Do you have a tissue?"

He searched through his pockets. "No, sorry."

"I really need a tissue."

"When I was in Boy Scouts, I found out you can use leaves for tissues."

She crinkled her nose. "Do scouts cry a lot?"

He cleared his throat. "Actually, it wasn't for tears we needed the leaves."

She shook her head. "That's more than I want to know." She put her sleeve to her nose and eyes and wiped. "Sorry. I don't usually do that."

"It's not a problem," he said.

She sighed. "All right, Dave, I will marry you."

"You will?"

"Yes."

"This is the best news I've ever had!" he shouted.

They threw their arms around each other. "Me too!"

They kissed and started back.

Once they returned, Rachel told her parents they were officially engaged.

Her dad tried to talk them into waiting a year. After some negotiation, they agreed on a six-month engagement.

Back on campus, they found being engaged made it more difficult to avoid problems. The list of activities they couldn't be involved in became longer.

Five weeks later, during summer term, they met on a sidewalk on campus at noon.

"How are you doing?" she asked.

"Keep walking. Don't stop no matter how much I beg."

"I won't. How have you been?"

"I'm miserable when we're apart. And now I'm miserable when we're together, but for a different reason. I don't see how we can go on like this much longer. I want to be with you."

"Do you want to just run down to the temple and get married?" she asked.

"Yes, that's exactly what I want."

"I was just kidding," she said. "Is it that bad for you?"

"It's pretty bad."

Two weeks later Rachel phoned her parents. "Mom, Dad, guess what? Dave and I have decided to get married in two weeks in the Idaho Falls Temple. We do hope you'll both be able to come."

"It's impossible to plan a wedding in two weeks," her mom said. "What about the reception? What about your wedding dress? Where will you live? You need more time."

"We don't care about a reception. We don't care about anything. We just want to be married in the temple."

"Hold on. Let me talk to your father about this."

Rachel could hear her dad fuss and complain up to the moment her mother told him they didn't want a reception. "Really? No reception? Well . . . I think maybe we should honor her wishes."

"You're just trying to save money," her mother said to her dad.

"No, no, I just want Rachel to be happy."

A few minutes later she hung up the phone and went outside where Dave was waiting.

"Guess what?" she asked.

"What?"

"We're getting married!" she said, throwing her arms around him.

Just Facing Reality

[*This tale is a continuation of "Just Going Together."*]

On Monday night, a little less than two weeks before their scheduled wedding, and just after returning from visiting her folks in Oregon, Dave and Rachel talked while they did the dishes after cooking for both their apartments.

"When you think about us being married, what image comes to your mind?" she asked.

"Hm," he said. After thinking about it, he answered. "I've got it. Waking up next to you in the morning with sunshine flooding the room with light."

She smiled. "How romantic. Could we carry that image a little farther?"

He kissed her on the cheek. "Oh, yeah, baby!"

She laughed, put both hands on his chest and gently pushed him away. "Let's not go there." She began washing dishes again. "Okay, so we wake up, and a little later we go in the kitchen. In your mind, open one of the cupboards in our kitchen. What do you see?"

"I see food, lots of food."

"Good. Now go to the refrigerator. What's in it?"

"Milk, cheese, ice cream, chocolate cake, eggs, bacon . . . dill pickles."

She made a weird face. "Dill pickles?"

"I like dill pickles."

"Whatever. Okay, in your mind's eye, what can you tell me about the apartment?"

"Not much, except in the morning the bedroom is filled with sunlight."

"Does it have a bathroom?"

"Oh, yeah, sure."

"And in the bathroom I assume there's shampoo, conditioner, tooth paste, dental floss, and makeup? Is that true?"

"Yeah, pretty much. Oh, also, I see a rubber ducky. Is that yours?"

"One more question. Who's paying for the food in the cupboards, the pickles in the refrigerator, the toothpaste and such in the bathroom? And who's paying the rent for the apartment?"

"We are."

"How?"

Dave kissed her on the back of her neck. It was a diversionary tactic; he knew she liked it. He whispered in her ear. "How about if we go back to us waking up with sunlight filling the room?"

"What room are you talking about, Dave? We don't even have an apartment."

"I know, but we will. We'll get one today or tomorrow."

"We won't have much money after we're married, will we?"

"We don't have much now."

"But the difference is my folks aren't going to keep sending me money after I'm married."

"I'll get a job."

"I'll do that too. Will your job be full- or part-time?" she asked.

"Part time I guess, so I can graduate."

"What if that isn't enough?" she pressed.

"Then we'll take out a loan."

"Have you looked into taking out a loan?" she asked.

"Not yet. I've been busy with classes."

"I think we need to step back and look at this in practical terms," she said.

"You've been talking to your dad, haven't you?"

"No, but let's face it, he's had a big impact on my life. He taught me to prepare for whatever I wanted out of life. I don't see that happening with us yet, and that worries me."

He shook his head. "So, in other words, you're having second thoughts."

"Not about you. I love you madly. I just keep wondering if we have any idea what we're getting ourselves into. In terms of finances, I mean."

"I can't talk to you about this now."

"Don't talk then, let's just take a walk."

They held hands but didn't talk until, finally, she asked, "Are you mad at me for bringing these things up?"

"Not really. Are you having second thoughts about us getting married?"

"No, Dave, not a bit. I love you tremendously."

"I can't be like your dad," he said.

"I'm not asking you to."

"What do you want then?"

"I just want to know where our food and rent money is coming from after we're married. That's not unreasonable, is it?"

He pulled away from her and let go of her hand. "I've always managed to get by."

"It's not just you now, Dave."

"I know that."

"I have to think about the children we'll have. I have to be reasonably assured they'll have what they need."

"You don't trust me, do you? That's what this is about, isn't it?" he said.

"I think we just need to do our homework, that's all. That's what living in my family has taught me. My dad used to spend hours planning a one-week vacation. I think we might want to take a few days planning our life."

"This gets complicated, doesn't it?"

"It's looking that way." She kissed him on the cheek. "But, you know what? I know we'll figure it out."

The next morning at six thirty, he called and woke her up. "Why are we beating ourselves up over this? I'm pretty sure your dad will help me with this if I ask him."

"You're going to ask my dad for help?" she asked.

"How bad could it be? I'll phone him right now."

"Oh, wow!"

"What?"

"You must really love me to phone my dad and talk to him about financial planning."

"Piece of cake."

A few minutes later Dave made the phone call.

The phone rang once. "Yes?"

"Hi Dad. It's Dave."

"You must have the wrong number." Rachel's dad said, and then hung up.

Dave wiped the sweat from his face and punched in the numbers again.

"What?"

"This is Dave. I'm engaged to your daughter. Oh, and just in case you've forgotten, your daughter's name is Rachel."

"You think I don't know my daughter's name, is that what you think?"

"No, but I'm not sure you know my name. I'm Dave, the guy who's going to marry Rachel."

"I know who you are! Who could forget something like that? Why are you calling? What have you done now?"

"What have I done? What kind of a question is that? You think I've done something?"

"Why are you calling me this time of the day?" Rachel's dad practically shouted.

"I'm calling to ask you for advice."

"What kind of advice?"

"Rachel told me how much time you put into planning for your family. For some reason, she thinks that was a good thing. She'd like us to do the same kind of planning for when we're married."

"It's about time you two faced reality."

"Look, I don't want a lecture. Just tell me what to do."

"Just like that?"

"Is this not a good time? I can call back later tonight."

"What I have to teach you can't be taught over the phone in a few minutes."

"I can call every morning if that'd help."

"Hold on please."

Five minutes later Rachel's dad returned to the phone. "I'll be flying out tomorrow morning. Pick me up at the Idaho Falls airport at nine-thirty. I'll leave twenty-four hours later."

"Where will you be staying?"

"I'll be staying with you."

Dave gulped. "You will?"

"Do you have a spare bed?"

"Well, yeah, we do. But the mattresses here aren't very good. I'm sure you'd be more comfortable in a motel. I could get you a reservation."

"I'll be staying with you."

"Yes, sir."

"Oh, one thing. From the time I arrive, for twenty-four hours, I want exclusive time with you."

"I have classes."

"You'll miss them then, won't you? This is my time with you. I don't even want Rachel to know I'm coming."

"You don't want to spend time with Rachel? Why's that?"

"You're the one who so desperately needs help. Twenty-four hours, and I'll be gone. I just hope you're still standing by the time I leave."

The next morning Dave picked up Rachel's dad at the airport. A few minutes later they approached Dave's car in the short-term parking lot.

"How much mileage on this?" he asked as Dave unlocked the trunk and tossed in a carry- on bag.

"There's about one hundred and ten thousand miles on it."

"Open up the hood."

"Here?"

"Yes, here!"

"Yes sir." Dave opened the hood.

"The battery terminals need cleaning. I'll show you how to do that." He pulled out a tissue and pulled out the dip stick, wiped it off with the tissue, and shoved it back in, then withdrew it to check the oil. "You're a quart low. When's the last time you checked it?"

"Last week when I filled it."

He got down on his knees and peered at the bottom side of the engine. "Do you know you've got an oil leak?"

"Yeah, sure, it leaves a mark on the driveway where I park it at night."

He stood up and wiped his hands and gave the oily tissue to Dave. "Take care of this."

"You want me to put it a scrapbook? It's your tissue. You take care of it."

Rachel's dad walked it to a waste container, came back and got in the car.

As they left the airport, he talked about car maintenance. On a legal pad, he wrote down notes so Dave would have a record of what he'd said.

As they passed the Idaho Falls Temple, Rachel's dad called out. "Is that where you're going to be married?"

"Yes."

"Let's go through a session."

"Now?"

"Yes, now. Why not? I'm not satisfied in my mind you have any idea of what it means to get married in the temple."

"I'm not dressed to go to the temple."

"And that's my fault?"

"I like to be wearing a white shirt and a tie when I enter the temple."

"I've got a white shirt and a tie in my luggage you can use."

Dave shrugged and turned off on the street that would take them to the temple.

"You do have a recommend, don't you?" Rachel's dad asked.

"Yes, sir, I do."

"Are you worthy of it?"

"I am."

"Well, that's one thing you've got going for you."

They went through an endowment session and then spent a few minutes in the Celestial Room.

"Let me give you a little bit of advice."

Dave felt less resentful of Rachel's dad now. "All right."

"I know it's easy to get caught up in the excitement of getting married, but try not to lose sight of the fact that you two will be making a sacred covenant with each other and with God. Also, when she receives her endowments in the temple, she will be taking upon her additional covenants. Please take time to prepare for and reflect on these sacred experiences."

"We'll do that. Thanks."

While they had lunch in the temple cafeteria, they had more time to talk.

It was then that Dave realized Rachel's dad was trying his best to help him be a good husband and father. It was hard to fault him for that.

On their way to Rexburg, Rachel's dad asked a question which threatened to destroy the harmony they'd felt in the temple. "Have you and Rachel picked out an apartment yet?"

"Not yet."

"You're scheduled to get married in less than two weeks, and you don't have an apartment?"

"We've looked at five places but we haven't decided on which one we want."

"I'd like to see them all."

Dave glanced at his watch. Just nineteen hours left before he goes, he thought. He didn't like the idea of her dad picking out their apartment for them but decided to at least let him look at them.

They first visited Dave's favorite apartment of the five. "What do you like most about this place?"

"Well, the windows face east, so in the morning, the sun will fill the room."

Rachel's dad looked at him and frowned. "So?"

"I don't know. I just . . . you know . . . thought it would be. . . ." Dave couldn't say the word romantic to this man.

"Thought it would be what?"

"I was thinking of the passive solar heating advantage of the place."

Rachel's dad suppressed a grin. "Yes, I'm sure that was what you were thinking. Let's go look at the other places."

As they visited each apartment, Rachel's dad had him rate each apartment in terms of cost, distance to campus, and if they would have to lease the apartment for an extended time or could just pay rent from month to month.

Finally they were done.

"I think with this information you and Rachel will be able to make an intelligent decision about which place to take."

"Which one would you pick?"

"It's for you and Rachel to decide, not me."

"Well, give me a hint."

"I'll tell you one thing. The place with the sunshine in the morning is way too expensive."

Dave felt his dream slipping away.

"If you want to wake up with Rachel next to you in a sunny room after you're married, then spend a night in a motel, but don't let that notion prevent you from getting a cheaper apartment that very likely will save you hundreds of dollars over the course of your time in school."

Dave's mouth dropped open. He was shocked that Rachel's dad could see why Dave waking up next to Rachel in a sunny room could possibly be a romantic experience.

When they stopped by Dave's apartment, there were three messages from Rachel. Dave listened to them while her dad was in the bathroom.

First message: "Dave, where are you? I went to meet you after your two o'clock class, but you weren't there. Call me."

Second message: "Dave, call me. We need to decide on an apartment. I'm getting a little worried we're not going to get a place. Love you."

Third message: "Dave, will you please call me? We really need to get together and talk. I'm beginning to wonder if maybe we should postpone our wedding a month or two. I'm not sure we're prepared to get married. Please call me."

Her dad came out of the bathroom and heard the last message.

Dave turned to him. "You think she's right, don't you?"

"You and Rachel are not just preparing for a wedding, you're preparing for a life together. There's more to it than ordering a cake and sending out invitations. "

"I'm beginning to see that."

Rachel's dad had his legal pad with him. "Let's talk about budgeting now."

"I should call Rachel. I don't want her to worry."

"Oh, when you talk to her, go ahead and make arrangements to see her later tonight. Let's say from eight to ten. Just don't tell her I'm here."

Dave phoned Rachel and arranged to visit her at eight.

After he hung up, he said, "I still don't understand why you don't want her to know you're here."

"You'll understand why after I've left."

Dave thought Rachel's dad would take him out for dinner, but that's not what happened. They made themselves scrambled-egg sandwiches. It was a first for Dave.

"How much did that cost us?"

"I don't know."

"Well, how much is a dozen eggs?"

Dave shrugged. "I never pay much attention to the price of eggs."

"I do. I can tell you the price of bread, the price of eggs, the price of hamburger."

"Well, that's great. Everyone needs a hobby."

At first Rachel's dad glared at him, but then burst out laughing. "Good answer, Dave, good answer."

After they ate, they talked about budgeting. By the time it was over, two sheets of the legal pad were filled with numbers and Dave's mind was whirling.

"Now let's talk about employment opportunities. You need a better job."

"There's not that many jobs listed."

"If you wait for a job to be listed, you're too late."

"But . . . ."

"Pick out twenty jobs you'd like to have, go there, ask to meet with the manager. Tell him or her about your qualifications. Explain that you realized there are no openings now but you'd like to be considered when there is. That's how you can get the job you want."

At eight o'clock Dave knocked on Rachel's door.

"We need to decide on where we're going to live after we get married," she said as soon as she opened the door.

"I know."

"Do you still want the one with the sunshine in the morning?"

He sighed. "No, it's too expensive."

She looked surprised. "You don't care about us being in that room when the sunshine floods into the room?"

"If that's what we want, then after we're married, we'll get a motel room for a night with a window that faces east. We'll enjoy the experience, but that apartment is too expensive for us."

She put her hand on his forehead. "Who are you, and what have you done with Dave?"

"I'm just saying we have to be careful how we spend the money we get."

"I agree," she said.

Instead of holding hands and taking a walk, they sat at the kitchen table and established a budget.

After that, they decided on an apartment. "I'll call the landlord and tell him we want it," Dave said.

"O.K.! Gosh, we've accomplished so much tonight! This has been so great. It reminds me of how my mom and dad make decisions about our family."

Dave tried not to laugh. "I'm sure it does."

He called the landlord from Rachel's apartment. They spoke a bit, then he put his hand over the phone and said, "Rachel, he wants to know when we'll need the apartment."

"Well, right after we get married."

"Yeah, right. It's just that I'm wondering if we should postpone the wedding, like you said on your voice-mail."

She gave a tiny gasp and then, to hide it, put her hand to her mouth. "Oh . . . ."

"Can I get back to you?" he asked the landlord.

When he hung up, Rachel was misty-eyed.

Dave looked at his watch. It was ten o'clock. Her dad expected him back.

"I need to go now."

"No, we need to talk. What's happened? Why, all of a sudden, are you thinking about postponing our wedding?"

"Rachel, you were the one who mentioned it."

"But that was because we didn't even have a place to live. Now we do, so why do you want to postpone it now? Is that all you want, Dave? Or are you having second thoughts?"

He tried to assure her he still wanted to marry her but that he could see they might need some more time to prepare. "This is a big deal,

Rachel. We're not just planning a wedding, we're planning a life together."

He gave her a quick hug and then left.

When he returned to his apartment, her dad taught him about the blessings that come from paying tithing, and, also, the advantages of investing a part of their income even when they were poor.

The next morning, on the way to the airport, Rachel's dad told him how to balance Church callings with family life.

Finally, just before going through security, Rachel's dad shook his hand. "Thank you for spending this time with me. I feel much better about you now. Welcome to the family, Son."

Their handshake became a hug.

"Thanks, . . . Dad, . . . for everything."

Rachel's dad nodded, waved once and took his place in the line for a security check.

The first thing Dave said when he saw Rachel was, "We need to talk about insurance."

She came behind him and put her hands over his eyes. "We will, too, but first a little break. Dave, I want you to go in your mind to our virtual apartment. It's morning and sunlight is filling our room, and we both wake up at the same time, look at each other and smile."

"We decided on a basement apartment. There's not going to be much sun filling our room."

She lifted her hands from his eyes. "We'll just have to imagine the sunlight. But, you know, the rest of that dream will come true." She looked at him as if she needed encouragement. "It will, won't it?"

"It will, Rachel. All our dreams will come true, especially if we plan ahead."

"When are we going to get married, Dave? We need to decide."

"I don't know." He grabbed the legal pad her dad had left him.

"Where'd you get that?" she asked. "It's the same kind of pad my dad uses."

"They sell them in the bookstore."

She gave him a reassuring grin. "You know what? You're everything I've ever wanted in a husband."

As he looked at the legal pad, he thought, Now I know why Rachel's dad didn't want her to know he came here to straighten me out. It was so we wouldn't be making these changes just because that's what he told me to do. He came here to teach me. And now they're a part of my life. Thanks, Dad!

Forty-five minutes later, Dave and Rachel used the legal pad to help them come to the decision to go ahead with the wedding after postponing it just long enough for them to make proper preparations.

It was raining the day after they got married. In their hotel room Dave woke up with Rachel at his side and looked out the window at the dreary morning.

He smiled. Somehow a little sunshine coming through a window didn't mean that much to him now.

Because now he had Rachel.

Olympic Gold

During the six hours Justin had worked at his uncle's gas station, he'd seen a gentle rain turn into a raging blizzard. The state police had already closed I-15 and he expected the same for Highway 89, which ran through his hometown.

Justin had been home from his mission for two years. He had been in his senior year fall semester at BYU when his uncle had a heart attack. Justin's aunt asked him to come down and take over the gas station until he could get on his feet again. It looked like it might be another few months before that would happen.

It was eight thirty at night and time to close up. Just as well, though, since he hadn't had any business for an hour. No cars were coming south from Richfield, and only one car had come north from Cedar City.

He was in the process of closing up when a '93 Honda Civic pulled into the station. A girl in her twenties, wearing a sweatshirt instead of a coat, jumped out of the car. The raging wind nearly blew her over.

Justin put on his parka and went outside to help her. "Here, let me do that for you, okay?"

"I can do it myself if it's cheaper," she yelled.

"Look, it's okay. Go inside and warm up. I can do it for you. I'm dressed for the weather."

She nodded and ran inside.

He filled her car with gas, cleared off her hood and windshield, and hurried inside. Even in a hooded parka it was painful to be outside more than a few minutes.

She'd set some candy bars, a jar of peanuts and a package of donuts on the counter and was looking for bottled water in the cooler.

He stomped his boots, took off his gloves and parka, and proceeded to the cash register. "Is this going to be it for you?"

She nodded. "How far is it to Salt Lake City?"

As he studied her face, his first thought was that she could be better looking if she wanted to. Her red hair was cut severely short as if she were trying to punish it for making her look good. Her amazing green eyes were wasted by the scowl she directed at him.

"Why do you want to know the mileage to Salt Lake City?" he asked.

"Because I'm on my way there."

"It gets worse north of here. There's a nice motel across the street. You could get a good night's rest and then see how it is in the morning."

"I could also scatter the clouds with pixie dust, but I'm not going to. I'm going to drive to Salt Lake City tonight.When they closed the interstate I decided to head north on 89."

"Well the thing is, it's no better on Highway 89 either. I just heard on the radio they advise no travel anywhere tonight."

"I've got to get to Salt Lake City by tomorrow morning."

"For the Olympics?"

She hesitated. "I guess you could say that."

"Let me guess, you're competing in the womens' bob sled team and you've dedicated your life to winning Olympic Gold, right?"

"Just ring up the gas and my food, okay?" She handed him her credit card.

He ran it through and waited.

And waited.

"What's wrong?" she asked.

"It's not processing the information."

"I can see that," she said impatiently. "Why isn't it?"

"I'm not exactly sure."

She paced back and forth while he tried running her card through the machine. "I need to get going," she complained.

"Well, you're sure welcome to pay cash."

She turned her back to him so she could go through her wallet in privacy. She turned to face him. "I only have three dollars and a little change."

"The food alone will be more than that. The gas comes to $28.57."

She gritted her teeth and returned all the food back to where she'd gotten it from. "Why can't you people have a card reader that works?"

"It's probably the phone lines out of town. Sometimes they don't work all that well when the wind blows. Like tonight for example. I'll tell you what though. My cousin Hugh and his wife Linda run the motel across the street. You can stay there tonight, and then in the morning after the storm passes, we'll use your card to pay for everything you've purchased up to then. How does that sound?"

"How many times do I have to tell you I have to get to Salt Lake City by tomorrow morning?"

"And how many times do I have to tell you that's a really dumb idea?"

"What is it, just because you're male, you think you're the only one who can drive in a snow storm?"

"The truth is I don't even drive in this weather."

She grabbed a piece of paper and wrote a message and gave it to him. "I, Carrie Carvel, owe this gas station $28.57." She signed it, dated it, wrote her home address, her email address, her fax number and her phone number, then handed it to him. "I'll send you a cashiers check tomorrow from Salt Lake City."

"Sure, why not? Folks do that all the time. Of course, mostly, they're locals. Not strangers from California."

"Would you mind if I get a couple of candy bars?"

"No, go ahead, get whatever you'd like. While you're doing that, give me your keys and I'll get your car started."

She handed him her keys. He put on his parka and gloves, got into her car and drove it across the street to the motel. Right in front was a vacant room, so he parked there and ran back across the street.

"What do you think you're doing?"

"I parked your car in front of cabin number two. Here's the key," he said, reaching below the counter. "We do this a lot of times. My cousin Hugh doesn't like his sleep interrupted, so he lets me rent out cabin number two when it's late at night. You can pay me in the morning and I'll make sure he gets the money."

"I'm not staying here, so give me my keys."

"Are you sure I can't get you to change your mind?"

"No, you can't. This is very important to me."

He nodded. "The thing is, I've got your keys and, for your own safety, I'm keeping them until the storm passes."

"Give me my keys!"

He shook his head. "Sorry, I can't do that. It's too dangerous for anyone going north tonight. With this wind, there's too much drifting."

"That's it! I'm calling the police!"

"Actually, we don't have police in this town. But we do have a sheriff."

"What's the phone number?"

He broke into a silly grin. "You want me to give you the phone number so you can call the sheriff and have me thrown into jail? I filled your gas tank, I gave you credit because you can't pay for it. I even threw in some candy bars. Look, would you like me to go the sheriff and just ask him to put me in jail? I mean, I'd hate to put you out any."

She glared at him, went outside to the pay phone and tried to find the phone number of the sheriff using the directory that hung from a shelf near the phone. But the wind was too strong and the pages kept flapping uncontrollably.

Justin felt sorry for her, went outside to hand her a piece of paper. "Here's the number. If you want, you can use my phone inside. It'll save you some money and get you out of the cold."

She grabbed the paper and brushed by him.

He stayed away from her so she wouldn't be intimidated while she talked to the sheriff.

"Is this the sheriff's office? . . . I'd like to report a stolen car." A long pause. "No, I know where the car is. It's across the street . . . What happened is that this Boy Scout stole the keys to my car . . . No, not a real Boy Scout! Look, are you really the sheriff? . . . Yes, I'm sure I didn't lose the keys. I saw this clown put them in his pocket. No, he's not a real clown! . . . No, he didn't run away. He works at the gas station . . ." She turned to him. "The sheriff wants to know what your name is."

"It's Justin Bigelow, Ma'am."

"Don't you ever call me Ma'am again!"

"All right, Carrie, whatever you say."

She returned to her conversation with the sheriff. "His name is Justin Bigelow . . . No, he's standing right here . . . I have asked him politely, but I'm telling you he won't give them back . . . okay."

She handed him the phone. "The sheriff wants to speak to you, so you'd better give me my keys or he's going to come out here and throw you in jail."

"Is that what he said?"

She lowered her gaze. "More or less."

He picked up the phone. "Uncle John, is that you?"

Her face turned a bright red, making her freckles even more noticeable.

Justin listened to his uncle and then began to speak. "Well, first of all, she's from California, so right away you know she doesn't know beans about driving in the snow. I tried to talk her out of driving north tonight but she'd have nothing to do with that. I got her set up with a room at Hugh and Linda's but she didn't want that either. So rather than have you go pick up her frozen dead body tomorrow, I got hold of her keys and told her I'll give them back in the morning after the storm has passed . . . Nice to talk to you, too, Uncle John. See you around, okay?"

He hung up. "Uncle John says he thinks you should stay the night."

"You can't do this to me! It's against the law!"

"It's for your own good."

"Listen to me, in four more months I'll have my law degree and I'm coming back to get you. This isn't over!"

"Come in May if you can. It's very nice here in May . . . or early June."

"Are you a Mormon?"

"Yes, I am."

"It figures."

She went to the window and watched the wind pile up the snow into drifts, shook her head, turned to him and glared. "All right, you win this time!" She grabbed the motel key and partly ran and was partly blown across the street to the motel.

Justin turned off the outside lights for the station and started to work up a deposit slip.

A few minutes later Carrie knocked on the door. He opened it. She had a towel wrapped around her head. "You were right. It is pretty bad tonight. The reason I came back is I need my keys to get my suitcase out of the trunk of my car."

He hesitated. She seemed calm, almost pleasant. He reached in his pocket and gave her the keys to her car. "Stop by in the morning and we'll process your credit card purchases."

She nodded and then left.

He was locking up when he heard a car start up. He turned to watch her speed out of town heading north.

He shook his head, drove to the bank to deposit the day's earnings, and drove home.

Fifteen minutes later he was in bed, but he couldn't sleep. The wind was picking up and he knew she was stuck in a snowdrift somewhere north of town.

He wondered what she would do when she realized there would be nobody coming to rescue her.

After a few more minutes of debating what to do, he got out of bed, put on his warmest clothes, got in his pickup, drove to the station, went inside, backed the tow truck out of its stall, filled it with gas, grabbed a box of candy bars and some bottled water, put in fresh batteries in his cell phone, got in the tow truck and headed north.

At first it was easy to bust through the drifts, but once he was out of town and in open country the drifts got bigger, and getting through them took all the skill he had.

Ten miles out of town he spotted her car, almost buried in a huge snowdrift. He left the truck running, grabbed a flash light and lowered himself down to the snow. He sunk up to his knees.

He fought hard to get to her, but there was so much snow piled up, he had to go back and get a shovel so he could dig out enough to get the door open.

She jumped out of the car and into his arms. He helped her back to the tow truck, opened the door so she could get in through the driver's side, then climbed in after her.

"There's some candy bars here if you're hungry," he said.

She sat slumped over, looking at the floor of the cab. "I'm so cold," she said. "My car quit."

"That's because everything got covered with snow. The engine couldn't get any oxygen."

Snow was rapidly covering the highway, making it almost impossible to turn around. He could only manage a few feet with each back and forth motion.

At first she didn't say anything but after she warmed up she started to sob. He didn't know what to say, so he just let her cry.

When the truck was perpendicular to the road, he backed up a little too much. The back end slid part way down an embankment. When he tried to pull forward, the wheels spun in place. They were stuck.

"Well, that's it. We're here until morning. I've got a winch in the front so in the morning, once it clears, I'll find a phone pole or a tree and pull us out with the winch."

She nodded.

He called home and told his dad where he was, and that they were all right and would be able to sit out the storm until morning. Grabbing the shovel, he went out to make sure the exhaust pipe was cleared of snow. Back inside he opened his window a crack to protect them from carbon monoxide poisoning.

"Why did you come for me?" she asked quietly.

"I wasn't going to at first. I went to bed for a while, but couldn't sleep. I knew you'd be real scared once you realized you were all alone."

"When my engine quit I knew I might die, and that you were my only hope. I wanted you to come, but I couldn't think of any reason why you should. I was so mean to you." She shook her head. "This is so crazy. Do you know why I needed to be in Salt Lake City in the morning?"

"No, why?"

"To protest against the Mormon Church. All my life I've been told that Mormons aren't Christian, but when I realized you were my only chance for survival, I hoped with all my heart that I'd been told wrong and that you were Christian, and that you would come and help me."

"I didn't come because of my belief in the Savior. I came because I knew you needed my help. It's no big deal. Anyone would have done it." He broke into a grin. "Well, anyone with a tow truck, that is."

"And lots of candy bars," she said.

"That helps too. Let's have one now."

They each had a candy bar and some water.

"We need to stay awake all night," he said. "So, do you want to talk?"

"Yes."

"What about?"

For the first time since he met her, she smiled. "What do you think I want to talk about?"

"All right, here goes. In 1820, a fourteen-year-old boy named Joseph Smith wanted to know which church to join."

At ten the next morning, a road grader came from town and extracted the tow truck and her car from the snow. She stayed a few days with his family, took two missionary lessons and then headed back home to California.

Six weeks later she called to say she was getting baptized.

In April she phoned to ask one question. "Is it nicer in May or June?"

"I'd say May."

"Why May?"

He laughed. "May is sooner."

Jessie James Alive and Well in the Wilderness

The first time I saw Jessie Carter, she spit. Lobbed it high in the air! It must have carried ten feet. Could have been worse though. It could've hit me.

"Jessie, this is James, . . ." Brother Tucker, my new boss, turned to me. "I'm sorry, I forgot your last name."

"Clairmont," I said.

Jessie suppressed a grin, turned her back to us so we couldn't see her smirk, and that's when she spit.

She was shoveling snow off the asphalt path that wound its way through the nature park at the edge of the BYU-Idaho campus.

"James will be working with you."

"Oh, yeah? Well, he's not working now. He's just standing around." She had a southern accent.

"Jessie, please say hello to James."

She turned and glared at me, "Hello, James," then started laughing hysterically as she turned to attack the snow again with her shovel. Her voice sounded raspy, like she hadn't talked to anyone yet that morning. "James Clairmont," she said, then started laughing again.

Brother Tucker shook his head. "I'm sure you two will get along real good. I got to be going now." He quickly handed me a shovel and a bucket of rock salt, and drove off in his pickup.

Watching him go was like being stranded at sea and watching the life raft drift away from you. I desperately wished I'd gotten the job

I wanted in the warm library, not outside in the cold with some lunatic girl. Well, no problem. I would work on the grounds crew until something better turned up.

I stood and watched Jessie work. "What would you like me to do?"

She threw her shovel on the ground and came after me, like she was going to beat me up. Not that she could. She was about five foot six and weighed maybe 120 pounds. I was six foot two and weighed 180.

"What do I want you to do?" she asked, her face thrust forward toward me. "Was that your question? What do you suppose I want you to do?" She grabbed my arm and turned me around. "Look around. What do you see? This is a nature park, James Clairmont. It consists of 22.6 acres of mostly wooded area, although there is a small artificially constructed pond which is filled in the summer. Winding through the park is an asphalt path which is exactly 0.9 miles long. When it snows, the path gets covered with snow and ice. Now, you would think that they would just close the park up in the winter, but, oh no, that would be too logical. The fact is that a wife of one of the vice-presidents takes a walk through this park every day of her life. And it is also true that last year she slipped on the ice. So since then, every morning in winter, the path is attended to. Do you know who does that work, James?"

"Us?"

"Yes, us. You and me. Although it is billed as a nature park, in the spring these same people plant wild flowers, and, in the fall, they rake leaves. The flowers may look wild, but they are not. I am one of those who does this work. You, also, are one of these people, but you won't last. No sir, you'll be out of here as soon as you can. How do I know that, you ask? Well let me tell you. Since I've been working here, nine guys have come and gone. They work with me until they can find another job on campus. And I'm sure you'll be just like the rest of them. So to answer your question, go anywhere you want where there is snow on the path, and shovel it off. That way we will never have to talk to one another, and that, James, would be my greatest desire. Any questions?"

"Okay, I'll go somewhere else and start shoveling," I said.

"Yeah, you do that, James. But don't just stand around. Work. Because what you don't do, I'll end up having to do."

"We're in kind of a symbiotic relationship, aren't we?" I asked as I started on my way.

"Come back here!" she yelled. "What did you just say?"

"I said we were in a symbiotic relationship."

"Are you talking dirty to me? 'Cause if you are, I won't have it! You hear me? Not from you! Not from nobody! I might be a little different than other girls on campus, but, one thing for sure, I am a good girl!"

I scowled. "You have no idea what the word symbiotic means, do you?"

"I ain't saying I do, and I ain't saying I don't."

"What's with using the word ain't? You are a student here, right? I mean, you do take classes, don't you?"

"Don't talk to me like that, you moron!"

"You're calling me a moron? At least I know what the word symbiotic means."

She leaned on her shovel, pursed her lips, then turned to face me. "All right, smart guy, define symbiotic for me."

"Symbiosis is the living together of two kinds of organisms if such association is of mutual advantage." I turned and headed off to find a part of the path as far away from her as possible.

"What mutual advantage is there between you and me?" she asked.

"We don't like each other, right?"

"Yeah, so?"

"We'll get done faster if we're always mad at each other," I started to leave.

"Wait a minute!"

I stopped and turned around.

"We might work even faster if we were within ear shot. I'll insult you, then you do the same with me. It'll warm us up and make us work faster."

I nodded. "Sure, why not?"

"The truth is, though, I can't call you James."

"Why not?"

"James is a sissy name. No self-respecting cowboy was ever called James."

I thought about it for a moment and then said, "How about Jesse James?"

She suppressed a smile. "Nice try, but it doesn't count. James was his last name."

"Hey, You're Jessie. I'm James. So we're Jessie James." She didn't seem to understand. "You know, Jesse James, the outlaw?"

"I know who Jesse James is, you moron."

"How are we going to do this symbiotic relationship thing?" I asked.

"We'll leap frog. You go out fifty feet ahead of me and start. When I catch up to where you started, I'll leap frog ahead of you. That way we'll always be within ear shot. Don't walk on the path either because it packs the snow down where your feet have been and makes it harder for me."

I trudged through the snow about fifty feet from where she was working and then started shoveling.

"I've decided to call you Sonny Jim."

"What for?" I asked.

Without slowing down her shoveling, she sang me the country western song, *Don't Come the Cowboy with Me, Sonny Jim.* What she lacked in quality, she made up for with enthusiasm and volume.

"So what are you going to call me?" she asked.

"Jessie."

"You can't call me that."

"Why not?"

"Because that's my name. We go by nicknames here."

"Why?"

"We just do. It helps keep things separate."

"Separate from what?"

"When I see you on campus, I'll call you Sonny Jim. That way people will know we're not friends and that we just work together. It's better that way. It wouldn't matter for me, but it might with you, when you're with a girl, and you see me. If you called me by my first name, the girl might think we were friends, when all we are, and all we're ever going to be, is co-workers. So come up with a name for me. Belittling or insulting is best."

"How about Wuss?"

She threw down her shovel and came after me. "Who you calling a wuss?"

"You said you wanted the name to be insulting."

She thought about it for a while. "I might, in a weak moment, agree to let you call me that, but some day you might call me that and I'll forget I ever agreed to it and I'll rip your heart out."

"Yeah, right. In your dreams, Wuss."

"That's it! You've stepped over the line this time!" She ran toward me and tackled me head on. We rolled down a hill. By the time we stopped, we were covered with snow. We sat up, looked at each other, and started laughing.

"Maybe I won't call you Wuss, after all," I said. "I think I'll call you Frosty, like Frosty the Snowman, which is what you look like right now."

She nodded. "That might be better. I seem to react strongly to being called a wuss." She stood, and on her way up the hill lobbed a handful of fluffy snow in my direction. "We've had our fun and games. Now it's time we got back to work, Sonny Jim."

"Where are you from? The Ozarks?"

"Why would you say that?"

"Because you talk like a hillbilly. And you say ain't? What's with that? You're in college now."

"I am from Tennessee, but I ain't . . . I mean I'm not a hillbilly. Where are you from?"

"Montana. Big Sky Country."

"Right. The only state in the union that couldn't think of anything to brag about except the sky."

Working together, it gave me a chance to get a good look at her. She had dark brown hair pulled back and secured with an elastic. Her eyes were also brown. Her face looked weatherbeaten, almost like it'd been chiseled out from stone by the wind that was always blowing at the wilderness park. It was a face with strong features, and it made me wonder if she looked more like her dad than her mom.

"Let me tell you something, Sonny Jim," she called out to me.

"What?"

"Nobody cares about the grounds crew. We could be out here in a blizzard. And they could've canceled classes for the day, and you think they'll send anybody out here to tell us?"

"If you're asking the question, the answer must be no."

"That's right. The answer is no. It happened to me last year."

An hour and a half later we were done. She looked at her watch. "We did good, finished fifteen minutes earlier than with any other guy I've worked with."

"What do we do with the shovels?"

"We put 'em away in a shed. Follow me, Sonny Jim. I'll never lead you astray."

A few minutes later she opened the shed and we went in. "Put your shovel over there in the corner. Just because we finished early doesn't mean we have to clock out early, right? Sit on that stack of fertilizer bags. We didn't use all they gave us last summer."

I sat down. "Is this okay with the boss?"

She shrugged. "Don't know. Never asked him."

"Well, I don't feel right about it."

"I don't care how you feel. The fact is you can't go without me."

"Why?"

"Because we're in a symbiotic relationship, remember? We work together, so if you're done, then I should be done. And if I'm not, certain people are going to start asking questions. And that won't do us any good."

"But it means we're getting paid and we're not working."

"If we work fast, we should still get paid the same as if we wasted time. Isn't that right, or am I missing something?"

"Well, okay, maybe just this once."

We sat across from each other on piles of fertilizer sacks. We talked for another ten minutes, until 8 a.m., then walked back to Buildings and Grounds to punch out.

"See you tomorrow, okay?" she asked.

"Yeah, sure."

We walked off in separate directions.

That's how we spent every day except for weekends.

At first, she did most of the talking and I listened. She talked a lot about her roommates. She didn't get along with any of them, and she had a long list of each of their faults, which she went over with me day after day. Most of the time I didn't say anything. Once in a while I told her I was sure they weren't that bad. She said they were.

One morning, about a month later, there was a break in the weather. We were raking and cleaning up around the flower beds when she said, "Sonny Jim, what's the worst thing you ever did?"

"What kind of a question is that?"

"You're not going to tell me, are you? You're afraid it'd ruin your, 'Look at me, everybody. I'm a perfect returned missionary' image. Well, you can relax because I know you're not perfect. Nobody is."

"I never said I was."

The next day, unrelated to anything we'd been saying five minutes earlier, she said, "I went with a guy in high school. He was a year older than me, and he had a car. His name was Billy, and he lived on a hill, so I called him Hill Billy."

"Does this story have a point?" I asked.

"Yeah, it does. In high school Billy and me, we did some things we shouldn't have."

"Do I really need to know about this?"

"I've got a question for you. Okay, one minute Billy and me are getting drunk on the weekends, and living on the wild side, and then, all of a sudden, he's filling out missionary papers, and pretty soon he gets his call, and then he gives a talk in church, and he's all, 'All my life I've tried to live worthy to serve a mission.' Except I know it's all a pack of lies. That boy had no business serving a mission. Smoke and mirrors, that's what he was doing. Smoke and mirrors. It's all just smoke and mirrors."

I sighed. "Why are you telling me this?"

"I'm thinking that's the way it is with everybody. So, what are you hiding, Sonny Jim? You might as well tell me, 'cause I'll find out sooner or later."

"I don't see that's any of your business."

"Did you have a girl like me before your mission, that you did things with you shouldn't have done?"

"No."

"Did you get drunk on the weekends in high school?"

"No."

"What'd you do then?" she asked.

"I worked for my dad after school. Then I ate dinner and studied. That's about it."

"What about the weekends?"

"I worked for my dad on Saturdays. And we went to church on Sunday."

"There's got to be something you're hiding." she said.

"Why?"

"Because there always is."

"Why can't we just talk about the weather?" I asked.

"Why talk about it? We're living the weather."

"Why did you open yourself up to me just now?" I asked. "And why do you want me to do the same with you?"

"I guess maybe because you're the best friend I got right now."

I felt guilty because, after work, I never thought about her. So how could I be her best friend?

"Who do you talk to about the things that are the closest to you?" she asked.

I shook my head. "Nobody. I don't talk to nobody."

By this time, I'd corrected her English enough she couldn't resist doing the same for me. "I don't talk to anybody," she said. "All I'm saying, Sonny Jim, is you can talk to me about anything you want. No extra charge."

"I don't have anything to say."

She shrugged. "Suit yourself."

The next day, when we were holed up in the shed after work, I took out a copy of the Book of Mormon.

"What's that for?"

"We're going to read it together."

"Not me."

"We can't keep talking about the same thing again and again. I don't care what your roommates said to you last night that got you riled up. If you don't let me read a few minutes every day, then I'll start clocking out when we're through."

"We have to punch out the same time every day."

I nodded, and opened the book and began to read out loud. "'I Nephi, . . .'"

She threw her baseball hat at me.

I kept reading.

She slammed the door on her way out.

I could hear her just outside the shed, telling me what a hypocrite I was.

Then I heard a car pull up, and she rushed in and closed the door. She sat down.

"What's up?"

"The Woman is here." By that she meant the wife of one of the vice-presidents.

She'd seen us. A short time later the door opened. A woman in her mid-forties, wearing a jogging outfit, looked in. "What are you two doing in here?" she asked suspiciously.

"We like to have a devotional for a few minutes after we've finished work," I said.

The woman spotted my scriptures and smiled. "What a wonderful idea! You two have a great day." Then she was gone.

"Good story," Jessie said.

"It's the truth. From now on, we'll have a little devotional after we finish work. It's either that or clocking out when we're actually through."

"You are evil!"

"Yeah, but in a good way though, right?"

"No, in a bad way."

From then on we read a chapter a day in the Book of Mormon. At first I did all the reading while she sat, shoulders slumped, head down, showing her boredom with every word.

Somewhere in Mosiah she offered to read half of each chapter.

One day when we were about to start Alma, she said to me,"I don't belong here."

"In the shed?"

"No, not in the shed, you moron, at this school."

"Why do you say that?"

"Because of what I did in high school."

"Go talk to your bishop."

"I'm not doing that. He'd kick me out if he knew."

"If he does, he does. If you don't go talk to him, you'll kick yourself out because you're feeling like you don't belong."

"I'm not going to talk to him, so just forget it, okay?" She swore at me and walked out, and I didn't see her until the next day.

While we were sitting next to each other, cleaning out a flower bed, she asked, "If I go to talk to my bishop, will you go with me?"

"Sure, no problem. As long as I don't have to go in his office with you."

"I wouldn't want you in there."

"Good. Then is it settled?"

"I guess so. I knew you'd say yes so I already made the appointment. It's for tonight."

We made arrangements where we'd meet.

At seven thirty we sat outside her bishop's office.

"Are you scared?" I asked.

"Yeah, I am."

"You want me to give you a hug or anything?" I asked.

She looked at me like I was an idiot. "That's not what you and I do. We don't hug. We just talk."

"We rake too."

"That's true. We've done our share of raking."

"Remember when I called you a wuss and you attacked me and we rolled down the hill?" I asked.

"Yeah, I remember that."

"Those were the days, right?" I said.

"Right. Can I tell you something, Sonny Jim?"

"Sure."

"You are the best friend I've ever had," she said.

"You know what? I think it's the same with me."

She leaned back and smiled. "I like it that we're best friends."

The bishop opened the door and smiled. "Jessica?"

"See you, Jessica," I said, calling her by her real name for the first time.

Twenty minutes later she came out wiping her eyes. "Let's get out of here."

We went outside and walked around campus. "You okay?"I asked.

"Yeah, I am. I feel a lot better. More like I belong here, more like there's hope for me after all."

"I'm glad."

"Thanks for getting me to come tonight."

"No problem. Can I tell you something that's kind of bothering me?" I asked.

"Sure, you want to do it now, or tomorrow when we're working?"

"Tomorrow's good enough."

She shrugged. "Whatever."

The next morning we found another flower bed to work on.

"You ready?" she asked.

"Yeah, sure. It's not something I've done that's wrong. It's something else."

"Whatever."

"My dad is an engineer. He owns his own company. I've worked for him since I was in ninth grade. I'm majoring in mechanical engineering here. I'm pretty good at it too. My dad is expecting me to come back and take over the company when he retires."

"Sounds like a great setup to me," she said.

"Yeah, except for one thing."

"And that is?"

"I don't want to be an engineer. I want to be a nurse."

"A nurse? You're a guy, Sonny Jim, you can't be a nurse."

"There's plenty of male nurses."

"It's your life. If that's what you want, go for it."

"My dad would throw a fit if I told him."

"So? You got to do what's in your heart, right?" she said.

"He'd quit sending me money for tuition and books."

"Not necessarily."

"You don't know him like I do. He'd cut me off."

"Nobody sends me any money. You ever hear me complaining?" she asked.

"Maybe I'll tell him in a few weeks."

"You going to be here all summer?" she asked.

"Yeah, I think so. My dad wants me to hurry and get my degree so I can work full time for him. What about you?"

"I'll be here. I'm trying to get done as soon as I can," she said.

"So we'll be working together through the summer."

"Looks that way."

When summer term started I was in a ward with people I'd never seen before, and I met a girl.

In the middle of May, while we were planting flowers, I said to Jessie, "I'm dating a girl."

"Oh?"

"I just thought you should know."

"Sounds serious."

"Well, it's early, but it's looking good."

"Sure, why not? It's about time you got married."

"It's nothing like that."

"Is she nice?" she asked.

"Yeah, she is."

She wouldn't talk to me the rest of the morning. After work, when we got together to read, she slammed the door of the shed on our way in. "It's not fair, Sonny Jim! It's just not fair."

"What isn't?"

"You decide to date a girl, and you just call her up, and get the job done. What do I do if I want to date a guy? Nothing, not a thing. Nobody in my ward pays any attention to me. So what am I supposed to do?"

"You need to fix yourself up more. Most of the time it's like you don't even care how you look."

"You are such a moron!"

"You asked for advice, so I gave it to you."

"You call that advice? That's not advice. You insulted me."

"You've got the basics to look good. You just need to do a little work on yourself. I mean, here we are working at a nature park, and we can't just let nature do its thing, we have to work every day. So, if we need to do that here, then for sure it stands to reason that we'd need to work on ourselves too."

"Who died and made you my beauty consultant?"

"Don't take it so personal."

"It is personal, you moron! I'm sorry I even brought this up."

"Me too."

She let out a huge sigh. "Okay, give me some specifics. Where do I start?"

"Back home my sister sells cosmetics. They have parties where you can learn how to put on makeup. Why don't you see if there's anyone selling it around here? Just do it, Jessie. What have you got to lose?"

Over the next two days she ranted and raved, but in the end she went to a meeting or a party or whatever they call it. A week later she was selling the stuff and doing demonstrations for parties. Not because she was that outgoing, but because she could get the cosmetics a lot cheaper that way.

She never fixed herself up for me though. Of course I could see why. Most of the time after we finished, we were all sweaty and hot, and desperately in need of a shower. So she fixed herself up after work, and we didn't usually see each other during the day.

In June she got asked to a big-deal dance. And I asked the girl I'd been seeing.

We bumped into each other at the dance. She'd never seen me dressed up before either, and so we just stared at each other.

"You look real good," I said.

"Thanks. You too."

No telling how long we'd have been like that if her date hadn't said, "Let's go dance."

I watched them go.

"Who's that?" my date asked.

"Just a girl I work with, that's all."

"The way you two were looking at each other it looked like more than that."

"No, we just work together."

On Monday I asked Jessie if she had a nice time at the dance.

"Yeah, sure," she said with little enthusiasm. "How about you?"

"Same thing."

"Great."

The girl I liked eventually told me she just wanted us to be friends, which, of course, meant we would never talk to each other again.

The first week in August, I got the courage to call my dad and tell him I wanted to be a nurse. He yelled at me and told me I didn't appreciate all he had tried to do for me. He also yanked all his financial support for my education.

I couldn't wait until morning, so I went to Jessie's apartment.

She came to the door.

"Can we talk?" I asked.

"Yeah, sure. Let me tell my roommates where I'm going."

I told her about my dad.

"I'm real proud of you, Sonny Jim. You had to do it, and you did."

"I don't know what to do. I don't have enough money for fall semester."

"Take out a loan. That's what everybody else does around here."

"I was thinking maybe I should go home and work for my dad for a year and save up the money I'll need to become a nurse."

"Yeah, you could do that. You think your dad will take you back?"

"Yeah, he will. He'll be thinking he might be able to talk me out of it."

"Well, you'd make a lot more money living at home and working for your dad."

"And it'd give me time to get accepted into a nursing program," I said.

"Yep. I can see you've thought this out real good. I'm proud of you."

"So I might be leaving real soon."

"Sure, no use sticking around taking engineering courses if you're not going to need 'em."

"Thanks for listening to me."

"No problem. That's what friends are for."

I hugged her at the door. It felt good. When our hug was closer and longer than either of us had expected, she pulled away and said, "We're not that kind of friend Sonny Jim. You know that."

"Yeah, you're right. See you in the morning."

"Sure, just like always."

We talked after that, but it was always like we were trying to protect ourselves from being hurt. Sometimes it was just like it had always been, but at other times we wouldn't talk much.

Two days before I was going to leave town, she came to work made up with all her fancy cosmetics.

"What's up?" I asked.

"You couldn't let it go, could you? You had to say something, didn't you? You are so predictable."

"I just asked a simple question, that's all," I said.

"It doesn't mean nothing," she said.

"Anything," I said, correcting her English.

"Let it go, Sonny Jim, just let it go."

"Just tell me why the prom queen showed up to weed whack."

"I'm not a prom queen," she said.

"You would've been one, if they'd had a vote," I said.

"You're out of your mind."

"You don't have to tell me if you don't want to," I said.

"Good then, I won't tell you."

After work, in the shed, she said, "We know each other's secrets."

"Yeah, we do. Totally."

"There's one thing you don't know about me," she said.

"What is it?"

"I'm not telling. It's a secret."

I cleared my throat. "Is it that you love me?"

"My gosh, are you out of your mind? Where did that come from?"

"Maybe it's because I love you," I said.

"It's because of my complete make-over, right?"

"No, it's just you."

"You love me?" she asked.

"Yeah, pretty much."

"And I love you." She sighed. "So what do we do?"

"I don't know."

"Me either." She leaned against the wall of the shed and stared vacantly at the ceiling. I moved over next to her and held her hand.

She looked down at our intertwined hands, then smiled and shook her head. "We're in a shed, sitting on bags of fertilizer, and holding hands. You know what that means?"

"What?"

"We're both morons."

"I know. We are. It's true."

"So, are you still going home fall semester?" she asked.

"You know what I think, Jessie? I think we're already home."

"Here? In this stupid shed?"

"Anywhere. It doesn't matter. As long as we're together."

She looked around the shed. "Yeah, sure, we could fix it up. Run in a hose. Get a propane stove."

"So, are you going to marry me?" I asked.

She pulled her hand away from mine. "Are you crazy? Asking a question like that here? If you're of a mind to ask me that, then you do it on an official date. And, another thing, you better bring me flowers. And not some you've ripped off from here either. I'm talking real flowers from a florist. And I want you on your knees. And I want music. And I want strawberries and ice cream afterwards."

"Well, could you at least give me a hint of what the answer is going to be, because I'm poor now and if I'm going to put out what little money I've got left for flowers, strawberries, and ice cream, I need to know if it's going to be a worthwhile investment."

She kissed me passionately on the lips, then jumped up before I could react. "Sonny Jim? You want to know something? I think you're going to be one happy boy! Yes, sir, in fact, I'm sure of it!"

After two months of marriage, I'm pleased to report that she was right about us being happy.

One other benefit—we're not in the shed anymore.

A Visit from the Fairy Godmother Over Prom Dresses

Let's get one thing straight. I knew from the beginning the whole thing was a dream.

I am Simba! Avenger of evil, protector of animals, a true friend to boys unfortunate enough to be named Jonathan or Michael or Ethan, boys with over-achieving moms who, because of their name, have to swim upstream their whole life. Boys who grow up to be accountants and such.

Okay, the part about being called Simba is not exactly true. My real name is Andrea.

There's not much you can do with a name like Andrea. "Call me And." I don't think so.

"Call me Andy." You say that and people will start calling you Handy Andy, and before you know it, you'll be getting phones calls from people wanting you to come and get their drain unstopped. So I've been forced to have people call me Andrea, which sounds like a girl who takes ballet and is learning to play the cello. Now you know why I'm mindful of all the Jonathans in the world.

What happened is a guy in my ward who is my age and goes to the same high school asked me to go with him to the prom. His name, oddly enough, is Jonathan. He's tall but not filled out, so he looks like a plastic guy from a happy meal that someone put on a stove and then stretched. He has a mom that is not doing him any good—he wears a lot of clothes that only look good in a Sears going-back-to-school catalogue, but not on a real guy in an actual high school. Jonathan is very sincere, and will do just about anything I ask, like, "Jonathan will you buy me a smoothie?" or "Jonathan, will you help me clean the garage?" He is in the gawky stage, but he has dark brown hair and eyes the color of black olives, and his voice has dropped an octave in the last six months. Also, Jonathan is very good about attending seminary and living the gospel. So he's safe, and, he makes me laugh.

So anyway, we're going to the prom in a week. Last night I went to the mall to shop around for a dress. My mom wanted to go with me, but I told her I just wanted to look around first, and on Saturday she could go with me to see the ones I liked the most.

I actually skipped school after lunch so I'd have more time to shop, and, also so I wouldn't be bothered by a bunch of other girls pushing and shoving each other for dresses.

There were a few dresses that would be within church standards, but, since I was by myself, and since I'm supposed to be in some kind of rebellious stage anyway, I tried on dresses I knew my mom would hate. I liked two of them enough to risk arguing with my mom that they weren't that bad.

For about an hour I was the rebel of my family as I, in the privacy of a dressing room, put on dresses I knew my mother would never let me buy.

The thing was, I wanted one of them very much. It made me look, well, different than I'd ever looked before.

I asked the store clerk to set aside four of the dresses, telling her I'd be in on Saturday to make a final decision.

Just once in my life I wanted to be thought of as hot—not my usual predictably-modest self. I wanted guys to notice me and talk about me when I arrived at the prom.

I wanted girls to hate me because, next to me, they looked about as exciting as oatmeal and raisins.

That's the way I felt when I went to bed.

Now here's the weird part. I had a dream. In my dream I was standing in front of a mirror in my bedroom looking at myself and wishing

I was more of this and less of that. Then I swear, all of a sudden, instead of seeing my image in the mirror, I'm seeing this old woman. She reaches out and grabs my hand and pulls me through the mirror into this huge prom dress store with racks and racks of dresses and mirrors everywhere, and there's nobody else in the entire store except this woman and me.

She looked at least as old as my grandmother. She had long white hair done up in a bun, and little circles of rouge on each cheek. When she smiled, one of her front teeth glowed like a flashlight. The dress she was wearing looked like it was from some Disney movie. It was beautiful, but changed color every few minutes. And she had a magic wand that she waved in my direction. I was afraid she was going to turn me into a mouse or something.

"Andrea, I am your fairy godmother over prom dresses."

I nodded my head and laughed. "It's the pizza, isn't it? I should never have pepperoni late at night."

"I am here to help you pick out a prom dress."

"So, basically, you're like a store clerk, right? Except you have a better selection."

"No, there's more to it than that. Because I have a magic wand, we can go beyond just picking out a dress."

"You mean, I can accessorize too?"

"More than that. You will be able to go to the prom in the dress you choose and see how it will be received by your friends. You will hear not only what they say but what they are thinking."

I scoffed. "Yep. . . . It's the pepperoni. I'm sure of it."

"What would you like to start out with?" she asked,

"Something my mom would absolutely hate to see me wear."

Before I could say another word, I was walking into the prom with Jonathan, wearing a dress that showed way more than my mom would approve of. I had to see what I looked like in a mirror. "Jonathan, would you mind if I visited the ladies room for a minute? I'll be right back."

"Go ahead, I'll just wait here."

Then, just as my fairy godmother had said, I heard what Jonathan was thinking: "This is embarrassing. I don't know where to look. And I hate the way guys are looking at her."

As I walked past one guy I heard him thinking, "I want some of that."

I thought the guy was just a pervert, so I didn't pay much attention.

Inside the girls restroom I looked at myself in the mirror. It wasn't that bad.

Suddenly my fairy godmother was standing next to my image in the mirror.

"You're thinking it's not that bad."

I hated that she was right. "Yeah, so?"

"It's true. When you're standing up, completely vertical, it's not too bad. But lean over toward the mirror . . . farther . . . farther . . . that's it. Now look at yourself."

I looked up and saw what Jonathan and anyone else who cared to look would see when I bent over.

"That's why Jonathan can't look you in the eye. It makes him feel guilty. He works hard to avoid pornography because it's so available these days. He doesn't appreciate you giving him the same views he's trying to avoid seeing."

I wasn't ready to cave in. "But aren't guys supposed to like things like this?" I asked.

"There's something you don't know about boys."

"What?"

"They're different than girls."

"I know all that, okay? I've taken biology."

"I'm sure you think you know a great deal. But there's something you don't know."

"What's that?"

"You think that boys react to things the same way you would, but they don't. It's completely different."

"You're going to embarrass me, aren't you?"

"I'll try not to. Let's use a cooking analogy. You've used a microwave oven, haven't you?"

"Every day."

"How long does it take to warm up some soup in a microwave?"

"A minute or two I guess."

"Do you know what a crock-pot is?"

"Yeah, my mom has one."

"How long does it take to cook something in a crock-pot?"

"All day. She puts the food in the crock-pot in the morning and it's done by the time my dad comes home from work."

"Very good," she said. "Okay, in terms of reaction to kissing or hugging or seeing someone who isn't being modest, a guy is more like a microwave oven, and a girl is more like a crock-pot."

I started to blush. "Why do I even need to know that?"

"You can't judge what a guy's reaction will be, based on how you'd react to the same situation."

"Hmm, so that's why that guy I passed on my way to the girls' room was thinking 'I want some of that.'"

"That's why."

"Oh." Suddenly my mom seemed much smarter than I'd given her credit for.

I was about to tell my fairy godmother I wanted to choose a more conservative prom dress when a girl came in from the dance. She looked like she'd been in a street brawl. Her hair was all messed up and her prom dress looked like someone had walked all over it.

"It's crazy out there," she said as she fixed herself up. "There's a whole lot of bumping and grinding going on! My date was so turned on. I had to come in to let him cool off."

"A guy is like a microwave oven!" I blurted out.

The girl turned to me. "What did you say?"

"A guy is like a microwave oven. You're more like a crock-pot, so be careful."

My fairy godmother smiled at me. "That's right. Good for you."

"Thanks, I just thought she should know."

"Why are you talking to the mirror?" the girl asked.

"I'm talking to my fairy godmother over prom dresses."

The girl stepped back from me. "I'll come back later."

She hiked up her dress in front, stood perfectly vertical, and quickly left.

"Fairy Godmother, I want the kind of a dress that I'll look good in, and that my mom and my dad will feel comfortable about me wearing."

In an instant I was once again entering the gym with Jonathan at my side. When I looked down, I was happy my dress was beautiful and modest.

"You look beautiful," Jonathan said. "I'm the luckiest guy in the world."

Strangely enough, I heard him thinking, "She looks beautiful. I'm the luckiest guy in the world." He didn't have to hide from me what he was thinking. And I didn't have to worry about bending forward or backwards or to the side. Anyway I went, I was covered.

"Thank you, Fairy Godmother," I said.

On Saturday my mom and I went to the store and, amazingly, found the exact dress I'd worn in my dream.

Someday I expect I'll be married in the temple. I expect Jonathan will be too.

Maybe even to each other. Maybe not. Anyway, we'll have helped each other along the way to reach that goal.

I am Andrea! And someday I am going to be married in the temple.

I Will Be Good for You

On the second Sunday in May, six hours after I gave my homecoming talk in my home ward in Draper, there was a knock at the door. My parents were taking a nap, so I answered it.

There in the doorway was a girl who looked familiar, but I couldn't remember her name or how I knew her. But whoever she was, she was carrying a large box.

"Yes?"

"You don't remember me, do you, Chad?"

"Not really."

"I'm Heather, Sarah's younger sister."

"Oh, of course! I'm sorry I didn't recognize you at first. It's just that you've grown up since I saw you last."

"I guess I have. I brought by some things that Sarah wanted you to have. Pictures of the two of you from high school, a couple of music CDs you loaned her, and all the letters you sent her before she wrote you a Dear John letter."

I thought she'd just hand me the box and go but she didn't.

"Can I come in?" she asked.

"Sure, I guess so."

Although I offered to take the box, she said she could do it. We ended up in the living room sitting next to each other with the box on a coffee table in front of us.

After two years, she looked more like Sarah now. Same blue eyes, her hair the color of ripe wheat, and a long graceful neck. Actually, she was probably better looking than Sarah. I realized she was now the same age Sarah had been when I left on my mission, but none of that mattered because I had always thought of her as Sarah's kid sister.

I couldn't understand why she hadn't left yet. "Well, once again, thank you. It was so thoughtful of you to drop these things by."

"Sarah didn't have much use for them after she started going with Ben."

"No, I don't suppose she did. By the way, how are Ben and Sarah doing?"

"Great. They just had their first baby."

"Really? Well, that is just so strange for me to think of Sarah being a mom."

"They're very happy together. Ben will be finished at Utah State in April and then they'll be moving to California to work."

"That's great."

"How long did she wait for you?"

I sighed. "Five months."

"Not very long, was it?"

"No, it wasn't."

"She was married six weeks after she sent you a Dear John."

"I know."

"She gave me the box just before she got married and asked me to drop it by your house."

"Okay."

"I'm sure she meant right away. But I didn't. I kept the box in my room."

"That's okay. I didn't need anything in it on my mission." I stood up, hoping she'd get the hint. "Well, anyway, thanks again. Maybe our paths will cross again sometime."

"There's something I need to tell you. It's a little embarrassing, but I feel that I had better say it now while I still have the courage."

I sat down again.

She looked away as if summoning up hidden reserves of courage. "The box helped me."

"The box helped you? How?"

"A few weeks after Sarah gave me the box, I started going with a guy. He was a member, but he wasn't very strong." She paused. "He wasn't a very good example of what a guy in the Church should be. But I was young and foolish and thought I loved him, and I kept thinking that because of me, he would change. But he never did. One night after we'd done some things we shouldn't have, I felt really awful and I couldn't sleep, so I went to the closet where I kept the box, and I started going through it." She stopped talking and her eyes misted up. "I'm sorry."

"Don't worry about it."

"I went through the box and looked at all the photographs of you and Sarah, and although I know I shouldn't have, I read the letters you sent her while you were on your mission. You were so excited about serving a mission, and you were so positive about her. And when I looked at all the pictures of you two together, I knew that this guy I'd been dating was not the kind of person I should be spending my time with. So, the next day I broke up with him."

"Good for you."

"From then on, I was very careful who I went out with. If they weren't as faithful and good as you, then I would have nothing to do with them."

"Well, how about that?"

"And on those weekends I didn't have anyone to be with, I went through the box. I did it so many times I have every picture and every letter memorized."

I felt very uncomfortable. "Isn't that something? Well, once again, thanks for bringing by the box."

She sighed. "It gets worse."

"It does?"

"In my mind, I became the girl who was waiting for you on your mission."

"You became Sarah?"

"No, I was still Heather, but I pretended I was waiting for you." She paused. "This really sounds like I flipped out, doesn't it? I started writing you letters. I wrote you every week until last week."

"I didn't receive any letters."

"That's because I never mailed any of them."

"You should have. I would have answered them."

She blushed. "I wrote them as if I was waiting for you on your mission, and that we were planning on getting married when you were released."

I felt very uncomfortable, but didn't want to hurt the poor girl's feelings. "I see. Well, how about that?"

From inside the bigger box she handed me a shoe box. "These are the letters I wrote you."

"Would you like me to read them?" I asked, not ever intending to actually do it.

"If you want. Not now, of course. It's a little embarrassing to admit what I did, but I just thought it would be better to get it out in the open."

"Of course."

"The thing is, you and this box are a big reason I made it through high school still a good girl, and still faithful in the Church. If it weren't for this box, I'd have never made it."

"Do you want to keep the box?"

"No, not now. I don't need it now. Can you believe it? I'm almost a sophomore at BYU."

"Are you serious?"

"I'll be taking classes this summer, so next fall I will be a sophomore."

"That is amazing. Little Heather is now a year ahead of me in college. I'll be going to BYU in January. Maybe we'll run into each other sometime."

She shook her head. "I'm sure I've freaked you out, and the last thing in the world you'd want is to see me again. But it'll be okay. BYU is a big place. I'm sure we'll never see each other again."

I showed her to the door.

"There is one more thing," she said.

"Yes?"

"This is the part I wasn't sure I could say or not."

"Yes?"

She lowered her gaze. "The truth is . . . I love you more than any guy I've ever known before."

I nervously wiped my brow. "I see. Well, isn't that something? I wasn't expecting that."

She patted my arm. "Don't worry. I'm not going to stalk you or anything. I know this sounds dumb, but the truth is, it's over between us. I guess the reason I came here and talked to you about this is because . . ."

"Yes?"

"Well, this may seem dumb, but when you were on your mission, and I was imagining we were in love, and that some day we'd get married, well, I felt I had a responsibility to be a good girl so that when you came back from your mission I could honestly tell you that I'd lived in such a way that I was worthy of a temple recommend." She looked at me and smiled. "I did that, Chad. Thanks to you."

"Good for you. I'm proud of you."

"And, of course, I trusted you to live the way you've been taught."

"Yes, of course."

"So now you have the box. I think having it means you have a responsibility to the girl you're going to marry to live in such a way that you will be temple worthy. So I'm giving you the box. It helped me. Maybe it will help you."

She kissed me on the cheek and then quickly left.

My mom asked who was at the door.

"Sarah's sister. I think she said her name was Heather. Anyway, she brought over some pictures and things Sarah wanted me to have."

"Heather is a darling girl, isn't she?"

I shrugged. "She seems a little scary to me."

That night I read all the letters Heather had written to me. When I finished, I felt a strong conviction that I needed to become the kind of person she believed me to be.

At the same time, I wasn't ready for almost a complete stranger to tell me how much she loved me. Especially my old girlfriend's younger sister.

And so I blew off her affection as of no worth to me.

I spent the summer working. In July I came home from a movie I'd gone to with some of my friends from high school. It was one of those movies where people say, "It's not too bad. It has just one really bad scene."

Once I was in bed, that one bad scene kept playing over and over again in my mind. I was disgusted with myself that I couldn't stop thinking about it. Later that night, as I sat all alone in the kitchen sipping hot chocolate, hoping it would help me fall asleep, I began to see how badly things had slipped since I'd returned from my mission.

I was no longer studying the scriptures every day. I still prayed but not with the intensity I had on my mission. I'd seen several movies which only had a few bad parts, and those bad parts were starting to take a toll on the way I thought about girls. I had started to skip priesthood and Sunday School because they were boring, and a few times I had intentionally showed up for sacrament meeting after the sacrament had been passed.

I was slowly reverting to the way I'd been before my mission. It was not what I wanted. I had gone through the temple. I had felt Heavenly Father's help on my mission. I didn't want to go back to what I had been, or worse, slide even further.

I wasn't sure anymore who I was, or what I was becoming. I just knew I needed to stop this downward progression.

A few minutes later while I sat on my bed, I spotted the box on the floor of my closet—the box that Heather had brought me my first Sunday back.

Bringing it over to where I was, I sat down again and opened it. First I read all the letters I'd sent Sarah. I had been so fired up about my mission. I wished I still felt that zeal and excitement.

I also read, once again, the letters Heather had written but never sent to me on my mission.

One paragraph struck me. "Please know that I love you with all my heart, and that I am trying to live so I will be worthy to be married in the temple someday. Please know that I admire the dedication you have to Heavenly Father. I know you will always carry that love and that you will always honor your priesthood and your temple covenants. That's why I love you and would gladly trust my life and my future and that of my yet unborn children in your hands."

After reading that, I wanted to re-dedicate myself to live the way I'd promised to when I first went through the temple for my own endowment.

I wanted to write down some goals. The easiest way for me to do that was to answer Heather's letter.

In my letter to her I wrote, "I've slipped a little since coming back from my mission, but I'll do better from now on. I'll go to the temple more often. I'll spend more time reading the scriptures and praying. I'll try to be a better home teacher, and I'll try to take an active part in my Sunday School and priesthood classes."

For the next few months, I wrote a letter to Heather once a week. Of course I never mailed the letters, but writing them helped me stay focused and dedicated.

In January I moved to Provo. I stayed in an apartment with five other guys, none of whom I'd ever met before.

I had no intention of ever contacting Heather. She was much too young for me, and besides, she reminded me too much of Sarah.

In the middle of February, however, something happened. The night before, I'd written a letter to Heather. Just as I'd done for weeks, I put the letter into an envelope and addressed it. Instead of putting it in the box like I usually did though, I left it on my desk because the phone rang and my home teaching companion reminded me we had an appointment and I was already five minutes late.

At any rate, I didn't put the letter in the box. And when I came home it wasn't there, so I didn't think about it.

Until two days later, when I suddenly realized it should have been on my desk, but wasn't. When I asked my roommate about it, he said, "Oh, I mailed it for you."

"There were no stamps on it."

"I put a stamp on it. No problem."

I was in shock. "You mailed my letter to Heather?"

"Yeah, any problem with that?"

"It wasn't a letter I wanted to be mailed!"

"Then you're even more messed up than I thought," he joked, and left the room.

I got Heather on the line.

"Did you get a letter in the mail from me?"

"Yes, I did."

"Have you read it yet?"

"Yes, I have."

"I'll be right over!"

She met me at the door. I was surprised by her appearance. She seemed just like the girls in my ward. That is, she didn't seem like a little kid anymore. More like just another student. Like we were now on an equal basis.

How can a few months of college do that to a person? I wasn't sure, but it had. I realized I'd gone out with girls in my ward who were the same age as Heather, so in my mind, that made Heather older.

Now it was my turn to be embarrassed. I explained to her how I had written letters to her, but didn't mail them in an effort to keep myself focused on doing my best to live the way Heavenly Father wanted.

She seemed a little surprised but, happy that she had been able to help me. "So, it worked for you too," she said.

"It did. Thanks."

"You're welcome."

She got a silly grin on her face. "So, Chad, is it true what you said in your letter, that you love me?"

My face turned a bright red. "I love the idea of loving you, as an abstraction more than anything else."

"Of course, that makes sense. We could hardly love each other because we really don't know each other."

"That's true."

She stood up. She now was the one who wanted to get rid of me. And I was now the one who didn't want to leave.

"Would it be all right if I came by once in a while?" I asked. "We could talk and get better acquainted. I mean, let's face it, we already love each other in an abstract way. Now all we have to do is get better acquainted."

She pursed her lips. "Well, that sounds great, but the thing is, Chad, I'm already seeing someone."

I nodded and stood up. "Of course, I totally understand."

She walked me to the door.

"Do you know what this feels like to me?" she asked.

"No, what?"

"It feels like we've been married, got a divorce, and now you're trying to get me to agree to see you again. What does it feel like to you?"

"To me it feels like I'm losing Sarah all over again."

"Tell me, what would I be to you if we did start seeing one another? A consolation prize? What you settle for when you can't have Sarah?"

I shook my head. "Sarah never made me want to be a better person like you do."

"She didn't try to get you to be bad, though, did she?"

"No, never. It's just different, that's all."

"What would we do at family reunions, with you and me and Sarah and Ben?"

"Uh, we'd all be polite."

She thought about it and then sighed. "Yes, that's what we'll do."

I thought it strange she said "That's what we'll do," instead of "That's what we'd do." But I didn't say anything because I didn't want to lose any advantage a misuse of grammar might be giving me.

She leaned forward and kissed me on the cheek. "We'll have to get a lot better acquainted, won't we?"

"Yes, of course."

"We already love each other, but we're not friends. I wonder if we'll fall out of love once we're friends."

"I wonder that too."

She playfully punched me on the arm. "You're as confused by all this as I am, aren't you?"

"Yes. What about this guy you're seeing?"

"Oh, he's just a friend. Which means he's ahead of you. You're not my friend yet."

"No."

"We just love each other," she said.

"It's not even that," I said.

"What is it then?"

"We love the idea of trying to be good for each other."

"Yes, that's it. It's a strange place for a guy and a girl to begin a relationship, but we'll just try and make the best of it."

"We will. We'll see where it leads us."

There was a knock on the door. Heather answered it. It was her friend.

She introduced us, then said, "Chad and I are in love. We may even get married if we can find out what each other's favorite colors are, and if we can make each other laugh and be happy."

"Does this mean you don't want to go to the movie?" he asked.

She scrunched her nose like she was deep in thought. "You know what? I guess it does mean that. I'm so sorry. Thanks for coming."

He left and we were still in the hallway.

"Where do we start?" I asked.

She sighed. "Well, with the basics I guess. My favorite color is periwinkle blue."

"Why can't it just be blue? Why does it have to be periwinkle blue?"

"It just does, that's all. What's your favorite color?"

"The color of your eyes."

She playfully punched me on the arm. "That is so cheesy."

"Maybe so, but it is true."

Bit by bit, day by day, color by color, favorite hobby by favorite hobby, we became good friends, and much to our amazement, fell even more in love with each other.

We were married on the last Saturday in April.

Sarah, who I had been in love with, is now my sister. Heather, who started out as my girlfriend's little sister, then became the one who made me want to do better, first became my one true love, and then only later became my best friend. And now she's all three—my best friend, my wife and also the love of my life.

We just found out there's a baby on the way. So now we want to be good parents for our baby.

Life is an adventure, and it's always changing. No matter the season of our life, with us together as a family, I'm pretty sure there will always be a reason to be good.

About the Author

Jack Weyland is the best-selling author of young-adult fiction for the Latter-day Saint market. In fact, the modern genre of Latter-day Saint-themed popular fiction is one he is largely responsible for creating with his overwhelmingly popular novel *Charly*. His interest in fiction began with a correspondence course in creative writing taken during a summer at BYU where he was doing research work. Since then he has published more than two dozen books, and over fifty of his short stories have been published by the LDS Church magazine the *New Era*. Horizon Publishers has published many of those short stories in several very popular book collections: *Forever, First Day of Forever, Punch and Cookies Forever,* and *Everyone Gets Married in the End.* Horizon also published his delightful children's book *King Daryl of Dread—A Christmas Tale.*

Born in Butte, Montana, Jack received a B.S. degree in physics from Montana State University and a Ph.D. in physics from BYU. Currently he teaches physics at BYU-Idaho. He formerly taught physics at the South Dakota School of Mines and Technology.

In 1983 he was given a Special Award by the *Association for Mormon Letters* for his contributions to the popularization of Latter-day

Saint fiction. Speaking of his contribution to literature, the awards committee said:

> *Weyland's gift for lively narrative, his ability to touch the lives and hearts of young readers, and his skill at subordinating a good moral to good prose and an exciting story have long delighted young and old readers. . . . Jack Weyland has blessed a generation with good stories well told, set in a real world peopled with the good and not-so-good but fathered by and centered in a caring God. Many of our young people are cutting their literary teeth on Weyland—and we should all be grateful.*

Jack and his wife Sheryl have five children and eight grandchildren. His hobbies include racquetball and singing.